Love Again

♡

Melissa Kline

LOVE AGAIN

ISBN-13: 978-0-9858134-5-1

DreamFusion Press, LLC
www.DreamFusionPress.com

Printed in the United States of America

♡

I dedicate this book to my dearest Grandma Billie, for if it weren't for her suggestion to, "go read the books in the attic," these characters would have never come to life.

Love Again

♡

Melissa Kline

"A first love always occupies a special place."

~Lee Konitz

Home ♡

Dillan Coggwell reached for the can of Pringles on the passenger seat beside her, keeping one hand on the steering wheel and a careful eye on the road. Another sign reminded her that she was heading west on I-84 toward Boise, Idaho.

Home.

Her neck and back ached, needing desperately to stretch out of the sitting position she'd been in for nearly seven hours. Even though she was exhausted, her mind was wide-awake.

What is he like now? Will he recognize me? Will I recognize him?

Her thoughts carried her to the next rest stop where she had a pee break, emptied her trash and took a stroll in the bright summer sunshine.

Dillan pulled her shoulder length blonde hair out of the knot on her head and gave her scalp a quick massage before throwing the golden locks back into a ponytail.

The day was uncomfortably muggy, full of humidity from multiple thunderstorms that had blazed through the northwest. Dillan was sticky from head to toe wishing there was a pool around to jump into. She stretched her legs out, took a few deep breaths of hot air, then got back into her trusty Honda Accord and headed for the highway.

This is it, the last few miles.

It had been five years since she had left Boise to go to college in Santa Cruz, California, one of the hardest decisions she'd ever had to make. Her life had been a roller coaster ever since, full of good and not-so-good experiences. Now, at twenty-three, Dillan was finished with her childish adventures and ready to be grounded once again.

A loud chime echoed throughout the car letting her know she'd received a text. It was Tyann.

Are you here yet? Are you here? You're killing me Di!

Her best friend's text being dictated in the monotone robotic voice made her chuckle. Thank God for the hands-free system her dad had installed last winter. She'd have had a million tickets by now.

"Aaaahhh! I can't wait to see you, Tyann!"

The high noon sun beat down on the city and the hills behind it. As bad as Dillan wanted to see her best friend, she *had* to stop in and see her family first. If she didn't, her mom would be heart broken for decades.

Where are you?!?!?!

Dillan passed the airport and found herself in the city on all too familiar residential streets. She rolled the windows down, allowing in a rush of smells that invoked bittersweet memories.

Collister Drive was hardly recognizable in full bloom.

Tree limbs canopied into the street and a rainbow parade of flowers dotted the lawns: a vast difference from the frigid winter months that Dillan was used to. The summer elements were a reminder of her beloved childhood, which didn't seem so far away. The feeling only intensified seeing Jan Powell's house looking exactly the same as it had for years. The sight made Dillan smile. She couldn't help but think of *him*.

What if he still loathes me?

The thought entranced her as she crept along the street, lost in visions from the past.

"Dillan! Over here!"

Her mother, Linda, stood a few feet from her car with an unusual twist of expression... confusion and excitement? It didn't help that her sun hat was tilted.

"Did you forget where we live, sweetheart?"

Dillan wanted to crawl under the dash. She'd nearly passed her childhood home going three miles an hour.

"No, mom. Of course not."

"Oh, I know who you were thinking about." Linda smirked.

Dillan tried not to roll her eyes. Instead she smiled, parked and stepped out of the car. She didn't acknowledge the cracking sound that came from her back when her mother embraced her a little too tightly.

"Oh, honey, are you okay?" Linda laughed as her emerald eyes filled with happy tears.

"I'm fine, mom."

"I've missed you so much. It's *only* been seven months, you know."

"I know, mom. I'm here now." Dillan smiled, happy to be so loved. She looked her mother over, noticing that age still wasn't catching up to her. They could pass for sisters.

"How was the drive?" she asked.

"Tiring."

"I bet. How does it feel to be back?"

"I'm not sure yet."

She looked at the medium-sized ivory brick house with brown shutters. Not much had changed. The old oak tree shaded half of the front yard. Dillan had read many books under that tree. The front porch was swept and clean. A decorative chime hung above the wooden bench and the evergreen bush, which sat just underneath the big picture window, was neatly trimmed.

"Well, you'll find out soon enough," Linda remarked. "Come on, let's get you inside."

The smell of the house hit Dillan with a raft of memories, bringing a smile to her face.

Home.

"Sista!" Nick yelled, running to give his big sister a hug. Three years younger, he was five inches taller, had disheveled, dirty blonde hair and hazel eyes, his features prominently like their father's.

"I told you!" Linda yelled from the kitchen.

"I thought Mom was blowing smoke up my ass," he said with a grin.

Dillan laughed. "Does she do that a lot?"

He raised his eyebrows and nodded.

"Are you taller? You are! And you're more filled out, too."

"Hell, yeah! Check out these muscles." He raised his arms and flexed like a goofball.

Dillan snickered.

"Yeah, I've been working out with Lan..." He paused. "The guys."

4

Too tired to figure out Nick's tongue-tie, Dillan playfully punched her brother in the stomach, and then went to the kitchen where she slumped into a chair at the small dining table.

Linda handed her daughter an ice-cold glass of homemade iced tea, which she happily sipped.

"Would you like something to eat?"

"No, I'm fine." Dillan smiled. "Thank you."

"Nick! Start unloading Di's car...please!"

He groaned, then grinned, catching Di's eyes before heading out the door.

"Where's dad?"

"At work." Linda joined her daughter at the table bringing a glass of water.

"He's working weekends again?"

"Yeah, we've been talking about fixing up the house and he's had his eye on a boat ever since his trip to Uncle Frank's."

"A boat? In Boise?"

"Well, he's got Lucky Peak up there."

"I guess."

"I'm just letting him have his fun."

Nick walked in with a suitcase, tripping over the carpet before heading back out.

"The neighborhood looks good." Dillan took a sip of her tea and rolled it around in her mouth before swallowing.

"Remember Emma Foster?" Linda asked.

Dillan nodded.

"She died a few months ago. Poor thing had a heart attack. Her family is trying to figure out what to do with the house. It's for sale now." Linda ran a hand through her short blonde hair. "The Roister family across the way

5

moved out… and Karen's daughter just had a baby."

"Really? Wow." Dillan smiled, feeling how truly happy she was to be back.

"I assume you saw Jan's yard?" Linda asked, giving Dillan a taunting smirk. "Right before you nearly drove past our house."

"Oh, shut up." Dillan teased.

"She's still going strong, despite her sickness."

Dillan, who had been sipping her tea, nearly choked. She grabbed for a napkin. "Sickness?"

"You didn't know?"

Dillan shook her head, still wiping herbal elixir away.

"I assumed Tyann would have told you by now. She's got cancer, just found out a few months ago."

Dillan's stomach churned. She suddenly wasn't feeling so well. "What kind?"

"Ovarian. She had some treatments that didn't go well, so now she's just letting it be, dealing with some pain. She seems to be handling it all right. I visit her a couple times a week just to see how she's doing."

The mother of Landi Powell, Dillan's high school sweetheart, Jan had been like a second mother to Dillan throughout her teenage years. She'd never imagined anything so terrible ever happening to the feisty woman who was so independent and full of life.

As Dillan's eyes lowered to the table, all she could think about was Landi. He had been on her mind the whole twelve hours on the road. Hell, if she were to be entirely honest, he'd been on her mind the past five years. A complete stranger to her now, she still couldn't help but feel for him. He was fragile when it came to his parents, having lost his father at five. Dillan knew that his mother's sickness must have been extremely difficult for him.

"I'm going to help Nick unload the rest of my crap and take a shower." Dillan stood, thanked her mom for the tea, and then gave her mother one last hug before heading out the front door.

♡

A little nap and a steaming hot shower later, Dillan was feeling like a whole new person, ready to take on Boise. She stood in her old room wrapped in a puffy white towel feeling like a teen all over again amidst all her untouched memorabilia.

The old No Doubt poster still hung above her bed, along with photos of friends and random cut-outs. The walls were covered in her adolescent art and posters; swimming in a sea of pink paint she had once chosen. A hint of her old perfume permeated the room, bringing her even further back to those times.

She sat at her vanity table staring into her emerald green eyes, thinking about the hundreds of times she had gotten ready in front of the custom made oval mirror. Lost in another time, she was quickly brought back to reality when a high-pitched sound came from the side of the bed.

Her cell phone.

She reached for her purse and fished it out, answering just in time.

"Hello?"

"Where the hell are you? I've only texted you a million times!"

"Ty, I'm sorry. I was just about to call you. I got caught up with the family."

"It's okay, I knew you would… But you're here! Oh my God! Finally. What are you doing? You *have* to come see me."

"Right now?"

"Yes, now! If you can. Jason's making dinner."

"I'll be up in a few."

"You better."

Driving up the steep road into Briarhill, a neighborhood of high-class homes that overlooked the city, Dillan was eager to see her best friend, Tyann. After meeting in a day care center at a young age, they had become inseparable and in a way were like sisters. Dillan's move had been hard for both of them but they managed to talk almost daily and kept each other up on everything.

The beautiful, modern stone home looked perfect as always with its professionally landscaped yard, wrap around deck, a myriad of windows of all shapes and sizes and a fresh coat of paint. Everything was where it should be, including Tyann's new Lexus sitting in the driveway, right next to Jason's newest BMW.

Dillan had just shut her car door when Tyann ran out of the house to give her beloved friend a hug. They squealed and giggled like schoolgirls, then took a step back to look at each other.

"God you make me sick!" Dillan laughed. "How is it that every time I see you, you look even younger and prettier?"

Supermodel-esque, Tyann was an exotic mix of Spanish, Hawaiian and French with big dark eyes, long, thick brown hair and naturally tan skin, complete with a cute petite body. She would look like a million bucks wearing a burlap sack.

"What are you talking about? You look amazing, Di. Seriously! I don't think you've ever been in better shape."

"I am so addicted to Pilates. Please tell me you

8

found someone to teach it at your studio?" Dillan asked.

"Not yet, but they have some decent classes at the gym."

They smiled at each other.

"I can't believe you're finally back, I'm so excited!" Tyann squealed.

"Me too."

"You are? Really? Cause you seemed kind of stressed about the whole thing."

"No, I'm fine. Now that I'm here, I feel good."

"Good." Tyann smiled. "You ready to go inside? Jason's waiting for us."

"Let's go."

The two friends locked arms and stepped inside the home that was just as beautiful inside as it was outside. They went to the kitchen where Tyann's high school sweetheart-turned husband was cooking up a storm. He and Dillan hugged and smiled at each other.

"You look great, Di," Jason said. "It's good to see you."

"Thank you. It's good to see you, too." Dillan stared into his ice blue eyes thinking he was even more handsome than she remembered. No woman in her right mind would think otherwise. Jason had an intense, masculine presence and the looks to match.

He ran a hand through his stylishly spiked dark hair before heading for the refrigerator.

"You want a beer? Some iced tea?"

"Iced tea sounds good."

As she watched him pour the auburn liquid into a glass, she couldn't help but think of Landi. It took everything she had not to bring up the subject.

"So... you want a tour?" Jason asked, flashing a

perfect white smile.

"Of course. Tyann's been dying to show me the new studio."

After getting her beverage, Dillan was whisked through the house to see the new renovations. Being the successful architect he was, Jason loved remodeling and customizing the home to their liking. The most recent project was a basement dance studio for Tyann, who ran her own studio in town. Dillan couldn't wait to try out some of Tyann's classes.

They eventually migrated back to the kitchen, where Dillan sat on a stool watching Jason toss pasta. She sipped her iced tea, while Tyann set the smaller table in the adjoining dining area.

"So what are you doing about work, Di?" Jason asked, turning to tend to the oven.

"I don't know. I have a few companies in mind for an apprenticeship. I've got an interview this Thursday and another next week. I'm just going to see what happens and go from there."

"Which companies?"

Having acquired a bachelor's degree in Interior Design, Dillan was eager to have a real career. She named off a few companies, getting an opinion about every one.

"Have you ever heard of FFC Interiors?" Jason asked.

"Sounds familiar."

"I've been working with them for a while, they're a really good company. I could probably set you up for an interview if you want."

"Really? That would be awesome."

"I'll see what I can do."

Tyann gave Dillan a sweet, knowing grin.

"Are you missing the kids, Ty?" Dillan asked, popping an olive from a nearby dish in her mouth.

"Terribly. But dance helps. So many of them have joined my studio, it's getting crazy."

"I bet."

Tyann's passions were dancing and children. She was a cherished kindergarten teacher by day – sassy dance instructor by night.

"So, I have to ask..." Dillan said, feeling her stomach flutter. "How has Landi been?"

"Not good," Jason said, without taking his eyes off of the salad he was preparing.

"Jan?"

"Yeah, how did you know?" Tyann asked.

"My mom. Why didn't you tell me?"

"We just found out. She hid it from everyone, including Landi."

"She *kept it* from him?" Dillan asked.

Tyann nodded. "I guess she didn't want to upset him."

"Poor Landi."

"Yeah, he's really struggling with the whole thing."

"When did you guys find out?" Dillan asked, not oblivious to Jason's solemn silence.

"Not even a week ago."

"My mom acted like it was old news." Dillan remarked.

"She's the only one who knew." Tyann said. "I guess she even took her to a few appointments."

"Really?"

"They've become good friends over the years."

Dillan frowned; mad at herself for not knowing.

After a wonderful dinner full of laughs and the best chicken carbanara Dillan had ever had, she and Tyann went for a drive on Hill Road – a windy back road just along the base of the hills.

Dillan let the wind whip her hair as she inhaled the sweet summer aroma in the wind. She looked over at Tyann who laughed.

"You seem happy." Tyann observed.

"I am."

"I'm glad. I was worried about you for a long time."

"I know. I'm good now." Dillan smiled at her friend. "So? What about you? Are you pregnant yet?"

"No, not yet. We're trying not to think about it so much."

"Right...That's why you talk about in practically every one of our phone conversations?" Dillan teased.

"I can't help it. It's exciting."

"I know. I can't wait to be an aunt."

There was a short silence as Tyann and Dillan sipped the milkshakes they'd picked up. Chocolate for Tyann; strawberry for Dillan.

"Is Landi okay?" Dillan blurted. "Jason seemed concerned about him."

"He's fine, I mean, he's handling it."

"Is he still with that twenty year old?"

"Beth, yeah."

"Are they serious? They've been together for what? Like..."

"A year and a half."

"Really? Doesn't she live with him?"

"Sort of. I don't know Di, it's like he just settled, you

know? You'll see what I mean." Tyann paused. "He's changed a lot since you last saw him. He's not the same old Landi, so don't expect it at all."

"What do you mean?"

"He's just different than the Landi you used to know, he's hardened, and his mom's sickness has only made it worse."

Dillan sighed, not sure she had the guts to face him again, even though she wanted to more than anything.

Diehard ♡

Landi Powell brushed his shaggy brown hair aside just before reaching into his pocket for his keys.

Tired from a long day of work, he hopped into his white Toyota pick up truck and started the engine, pulling out of Motive Power, Inc. for the day. He had been called in to work on a Saturday, which was not so rare in his line of work as a machinist. He didn't mind, anything to get his mind off of his mom... and now *her*. Zoning out while he worked had become almost a comfort and something he looked forward to, turning him into a workaholic.

Pulling into his mother's driveway, he couldn't help but glance two houses up, glad to see no unfamiliar cars, no signs of her.

Maybe she didn't come after all. Good. But what if something happened?

Landi shook his head and the ridiculous thoughts, then got out of his truck, checked the mailbox and walked into his childhood home.

Jan was happily watering her plants outside. Landi

14

took a moment to watch her before opening the screen door. She was as beautiful as ever, though a mere ghost of her former self. Her golden brown hair was thin and dull, skin pale, eyes tired. The youthful mother he remembered was long gone.

"Hi." Jan beamed, giving her son a kiss on the cheek. "How was work?"

"Tiring." He sat in a patio chair and looked out over the yard. "How are you feeling today?"

"Good. I've only had to take one pill so far. I feel great."

"Really?"

She nodded. "Mmmhmm."

Landi wanted to believe her but found it difficult. "Just be careful, remember what the doctor said? If you start to feel anything, anything at all..."

"I know honey, I'm fine."

He swallowed, hating the fact that his mother was sick. He still hadn't accepted it and wasn't sure if he ever would.

"So what do you want for dinner tonight?" he asked, running a hand over his hair.

"I think I'll just have some leftovers from yesterday's lunch. I'm not very hungry."

"You don't want me to pick up anything?"

"No, I want you to go home and rest."

"Well, what can I do before I go?"

Jan sat in a patio chair facing her son and leaned in with a devilish grin. "You can tell me how you feel about Dillan's arrival."

Landi froze. He avoided his mother's eyes. "I don't want to talk about it."

"Linda told me the news a few days ago. I saw Di's

car in the driveway earlier today."

"That's great, mom."

"Oh, come on, don't act like you don't care."

"I don't."

"You can't avoid her forever, Landi, especially now that she's moved back."

"Sure I can." He'd done it every time she'd come to visit, even with her attempts to connect with him. He wasn't going to stop now.

Jan shook her head and sat back in her chair. "Three years since you've seen or spoken to her and you still can't face her?"

"It's not that I can't, I just don't want to."

"You don't think the two of you could just be friends?"

"No."

"Why not?"

"Because, I'm done. I was done a long time ago. I don't care about her or what she does. Period. End of story. I don't want to talk about it anymore."

Jan knew her son all too well. He was lying, whether intentionally or not. Dillan had been the only girl he'd ever truly loved and she knew that deep down inside he was still wounded from her leaving him.

Together for nearly five years, the two were literally inseparable. Having met at the tender age of thirteen, both of them became the best of friends before falling deeply in love. Jan remembered being so frazzled and stressed over their involvement. She and Linda had been completely powerless over their diehard teenage love. She giggled, remembering the good and scary moments: watching them get into food fights in the kitchen, seeing them snuggled up on the couch, walking in on them having sex.

Despite it all, Jan almost missed those times, missed her son being the carefree, laid back person he used to be. It seemed a part of him had been missing for a long time. Jan wondered if her son would ever be truly happy ever again.

"I guess I'll head out then." Landi stood, agitated from having to talk about *her*.

"Okay, honey." Jan stood with her son and they walked into the kitchen. "Landi?"

He turned to look at her with frustration in his eyes.

"I didn't mean to upset you."

"I'm not upset."

"Are you sure?"

"Do you still want to go to the hardware store tomorrow?" Landi asked.

"Yes, if you don't mind."

"Of course not. I'll be here around noon, let's get some lunch."

"Okay." Jan hugged her son, squeezing him tight. "I love you."

"I love you, too. See you tomorrow."

Landi took the long way home on Hill Road for a change. He needed to clear his head.

How dare she come back.

He wanted more than anything to give her a piece of his mind. To tell her to go back to wherever she came from. It didn't help that all of their friends were mutual. Avoiding her was not going to be easy. It only made him more angry.

Why did she have to move back when he needed his friends the most? When his life was more unstable than it had ever been? If he ever did run into her, he would tell her exactly what he thought and where she should go.

17

He had lost any feeling he ever had for her years ago; she was merely just another girl who had broken his heart.

Landi was so consumed in thoughts; he almost missed the familiar silver Lexus just up the road coming his way. He smiled, knowing it was Tyann and positioned his palm over the steering wheel to honk when a flutter of golden locks caught his eyes. His heart jumped into his throat, causing his hand to slip. A blaring honk jerked him out of the trance.

Shit! Shit! Shit!

He ducked as best he could, sped up and quickly drove away.

The dark green, cozy home on Tenth Street was a welcome sight after such a humiliating incident. Landi pulled into his driveway and sighed, eyeing his well-kept yard.

He had always loved the homes on the north end and knew since he was young that he wanted to own a house there. Built in the fifties, his home was small with two bedrooms, one bathroom, a kitchen, dining area and basement. Beautiful wood floors and dark paint gave the interior a cabin feel that fit Landi and his personality perfectly. It was just right for him and made for a good project on a slow weekend. Having worked as a general carpenter for his uncle as a teen, Landi liked to put his learned skills to good use.

Stepping into the doorway, Landi took his shoes and work polo off, more than ready to unwind. He went to the kitchen, grabbed a bottle of beer then sprawled out onto his couch and flipped on the television. He was quickly sucked into a show on the Discovery channel when he heard a car pull up.

Beth walked in covered in shopping bags, her long

brown hair in a tousle on the top of her head. She set her belongings down and shook out her bun then walked to Landi with a grin, straddling him before leaning down to give him a kiss.

"Hi." She smiled and devoured him with those amazing lips. "How are you?"

"Tired, how was your day?"

"Fine, I had dinner with mom and dad then Erika and I went shopping. Momma gave me a new credit card."

"Another one, huh?"

"Yep… and, I got some goodies for you."

Landi pulled Beth to him and tickled her neck with kisses. "What kind of goodies?"

"I guess you'll have to wait and see…" she giggled. "Have you eaten?"

Landi shook his head without taking his eyes off of her.

"Good, I brought food." Beth started to get up but Landi pulled her back down, giving her a passionate kiss.

Beth was exactly the distraction he needed with her soft, supple skin, sexy, slender figure and full lips. It was physical attraction that had brought them together and one of the only ways they truly connected. Beth was smart, sexy and a little snobbish coming from a rich family, not exactly Landi's type. She always got what she wanted and Landi was no exception, giving him no choice but to give in to her seductive ways.

Beth wasted no time unzipping Landi's pants as she kissed his neck, slowly making her way down.

It wasn't long before all of their clothing was on the floor as they practiced bedroom gymnastics in the living room.

Obnoxious ♡

"**G**oodnight, sweetheart."

"Night, mom."

Dillan couldn't help but chuckle at her mother who'd said goodnight at least a thousand times since their family movie ended.

"Mom," Nick whined. "Dillan will still be here in the morning. I promise."

"I know, I just…"

"Mom…"

"Okay, goodnight my sweet children. See you in the morning."

Dillan and Nick smirked at each other from across the living room couch, bathed in the glow of the television still blaring movie credit music. Dillan eyed her brother's whisker covered cheeks. She still couldn't get over the fact that he was an adult.

Nick threw a giant handful of popcorn at Dillan, which started a war. They ended up on the floor in the kitchen half laughing, half shushing each other to be quiet.

Dillan sat up and fished popcorn from her hair.

"So Sis, I kind of have a confession to make," Nick said, retrieving his purple baseball cap from the floor. He ran a hand through his disheveled blond locks before putting the cap back on.

"A confession?" Dillan laughed, not at all taking him seriously.

"I hang out with Landi, occasionally."

"What?" Dillan was confused. Landi had always been nice to Nick when they were kids but she just couldn't see them hanging out as adults. To her, her brother was still thirteen.

"I don't care." She lied, laughing it off. "When did this start?"

"A while ago. His girlfriend and my girl are best friends so, I don't know. We just drink a beer every once in a while after work, sometimes we all hang out. It's no big deal though, right?"

"Right, no. I really don't care, but thanks for the info." She grabbed a handful of popcorn and threw it at him. "So how long have you been with this girl? Is it the same one from Christmas?"

Not that she cared… that much. Changing the subject was priority.

"No, actually I met Erika on New Year's."

"Erika?"

"Yeah, she's way cute and sweet, you'll meet her."

"Is it serious?"

Nick grinned. "I don't know."

Dillan smiled, hiding the hundreds of thoughts going through her head.

What did Landi's girlfriend look like? How could he

hang out with my brother? Why was everyone else a part of his life except me?

"Are you guys really good friends?" Dillan asked.

Nick raised an eyebrow. "Well, yeah, she's my girl."

"No, I mean you and Landi."

They both laughed, half eating buttery tidbits.

"Oh, um..." Nick stalled while Dillan fished the dustpan and broom out of the hall closet. She began sweeping up the popcorn mess on the kitchen floor as Nick rinsed dishes in the sink.

"I mean, do you talk about stuff? With Landi?" Dillan asked.

"What kind of stuff?"

"You know, *stuff.*"

"You mean, you?" Nick flicked water at her.

Dillan shrugged, feeling a little embarrassed. She emptied the dustpan into the garbage then bopped Nick on the butt with the broomstick.

"No. Honestly, I don't think you've been a part of any of our conversations."

She nodded. "Well, that's a good thing."

Was it?

"Yeah, I wouldn't really want to go there with him anyway, know what I mean?"

"Yeah." *No.*

Nick dried off his hands, snapped Dillan with the dish towel then stretched and gave a dramatic sigh. "I'm going to head to bed... text my girl. Love you sis, I'm glad you're back."

"Me too." Dillan received a hug then went back to the couch and slowly picked popcorn from the cushions. She couldn't get her mind off of Landi, knowing it was going to be a challenge to get to know him again.

All she wanted was her long lost friend back.

♡

"Di, honey?"

Dillan stirred and stretched, realizing her neck wasn't as happy as it had been the day before. She stared up at her mother who was beaming at her as if she was some kind of apparition.

"Your purse has been buzzing all morning. I thought I'd wake you in case it was something important."

"Thanks…" Dillan flopped back into the couch cushions, regretting it when her neck pinched. She fetched her purse from the coffee table and pulled out the phone she'd been neglecting.

Three missed calls and five texts.

Tyann: Good morning sunshine!

Terry: Want to get coffee? Call me.

Tyann: Thanx for coming up last night. I love you.

Terry: Ok, if not coffee – lunch?

Tyann: What are you up to today?

Dillan was just about to respond to her nagging best friends when the phone began to buzz with an energy she did not share.

"Hello?"

"Dillan! There you are! I heard you just got in… what are you up to?"

"Terry! Hey, girl. I was just about to call you."

"Sorry, did I wake you?"

"Sort of, but that's okay. I needed to get up anyway." Dillan yawned.

"Good, you can take me up on that coffee rain

check."

"Sounds good. Let me get dressed first."

Terry chuckled. "I guess I can do that."

Starbucks was a welcome sight. Dillan ordered the tallest, fattest, most caffeine containing latte her body could handle, then sat in an obnoxiously patterned oversized chair and waited for her friend.

Terry had been the shy meek redhead in high school that Tyann and Dillan had befriended their junior year. She had quickly become a part of their group, never really leaving it.

Dillan nestled deeper into the chair, just feeling the effects of her caffeine explosion when her phone beeped. She groaned and leaned over to fetch her purse from the floor when a pair of fire engine red toes appeared before her. She looked up to see not one, but two pairs of big blue eyes. Terry and her two-year-old daughter Tibby stared back at her.

"Di!"

"Terry!" Dillan stood and embraced her second best friend. "I missed you guys."

She gave Tibby a kiss on the cheek who immediately backed away, clinging to her mother.

"You probably don't even remember me, do you?" Dillan asked, looking around Terry's shoulder to see Tibby's chubby freckled face. "You were a lot smaller the last time I saw you."

"No!" Tibby said with a frown.

"Don't worry, she'll warm up to you again." Terry went to get a drink with Tibby on her hip as Dillan looked her friend over. Terry was still tall and skinny as ever, but not sickly so. She wore a navy blue halter maxi dress that accentuated her freckled fair skin and feminine figure perfectly. Her long auburn hair was braided to one side with wisps framing her face. Dillan smiled at her beautiful friend.

Tibby, who was the spitting image of her mother, peeked at Dillan making a game of it. She managed to get a game of peekaboo started with some giggles before her mother turned and joined Dillan.

"So?" Terry smiled, balancing her daughter and extra large drink on her lap. "Are you glad to be home?"

"Yeah, I am."

"I can't wait for us to hang out like old times. It's going to be so much fun."

"I know." Dillan smiled. "So what's been going on with you? Have things settled down some?"

"I guess, I'm still having a hard time. I think Jesse's got a girlfriend."

"What? Why do you think that?"

"Tibby's been giving me clues and I've seen an unfamiliar car parked in front of the house more than once."

"Oh, Terry." Dillan truly felt for her friend. Recently separated, Terry had been depressed for months. She was still madly in love with her husband Jesse, the father of Tibby, who was also an old friend from their teen years.

"Does he still take Tibby on the weekends?" Dillan asked.

"Oh yeah. And he's really nice to me, almost kiss-ass. I don't know what to think anymore."

They were silent as Tibby tried to slip off of her mother's lap.

"How's school and your job?" Dillan asked, hoping to bring up a lighter subject. Terry had been working toward getting an early childhood teaching education whilst working at a daycare full time. Just the thought of Terry's schedule made Dillan tired.

"Crazy, it's been hectic trying to balance everything. I get pretty run down."

"Does your mom still help you with Tibbs?"

"Yeah, but she just recently went full time at the floral shop so Tibby stays with me all day at daycare and… well, let's just say I don't get a lot of time to myself."

"I can imagine."

"Which is fine, Tibbs and I are total BFF's," she said, giving her daughter a big kiss on the cheek, which created the cutest giggle Dillan had ever heard.

"But you still need time to yourself," Dillan said, worrying about her friend.

Terry shrugged.

Dillan smiled at Tibby who was now playing with the pattern on the carpet. "Well, if you want, I'd be more than willing to baby-sit."

"I wouldn't do that to you, she's hard work."

"I think it would be fun. We could get reacquainted."

Terry smiled then grabbed a full sippy cup from the diaper bag and handed it to Tibby.

"So, I'm not sure if I should ask…" Terry started. "But have you seen or talked to Landi yet?"

"No, I'm a little scared. I don't know what to expect."

Terry nodded. "He and Jesse still hang out all the time. I guess Nick's a part of their group now, too."

"Yeah, I heard."

There was a short pause as Tibby laughed out loud.

"We should have a girl's night out and go guy

hunting," Terry said.

"That would be fun."

"Let's plan something this week."

"Okay, but only if you let me baby-sit."

Just then, Tibby splashed apple juice all over her mother and Dillan.

"You sure about that?"

"Yep." Dillan gave Tibby a knowing grin. "We're going to be the best of friends."

Pills ♡

Landi stretched, slowly waking up after turning his alarm off. He lay in bed for a while thinking about the day ahead, staring up at the ceiling fan blades whirling around in a blur. He found his thoughts wandering to the past. Memories of days he wished he didn't miss. The girl he wished he could ignore when the phone on his bedside table buzzed.

It was his best friend Jason… again.

He ignored his phone and the hint of guilt creeping in and headed for the shower. He'd been successfully avoiding everyone except his mom and girlfriend for the past four days. Pure serenity. Being a hermit was his specialty and he was proud of it.

As he quickly toweled off and slipped some boxers on, he heard the front door open.

Beth.

He grinned and walked out into the living room knowing she'd like what she saw.

"Hey babe…"

Jason stood in the doorway staring at him with a stone cold, deathly serious expression. He was in full on work mode in a crisp button down shirt, navy slacks, shiny shoes and stern demeanor.

"You're not going to do this," he stated.

Guilt surfaced. "Do what?"

"Hide like this."

"Whatever." Landi turned and walked to the bedroom where he slipped some beat-up jeans on then regretfully walked back to the living room to face Mr. Professional.

"I'm not hiding," he said.

"Bullshit, you're not. Why aren't you answering your phone?"

"I've been busy."

Jason gave him a cynical look. "You've got to face this, man."

"I don't have to face anything." Landi fell into his couch, playing it cool.

"You're scared, aren't you?"

Landi laughed. "Why would I be scared?"

"You're afraid you're going to feel the same way about her now than you did then."

"That's funny."

Was it? Damn Jason for knowing him so well.

"So what is your plan here? You're going to avoid her for the next three years? Hide in your house your whole life?" Jason checked his watch then crossed his arms.

"No."

"Good, you're coming to dinner tonight."

"No, I'm not."

"Do you have other plans?"

"No, but..."

"See you at seven."

"J! Come on, man!" Landi followed his stubborn friend out to his fancy car. "I don't have anything to say to her! It's a waste of time!"

"See you later." Jason got into his BMW and sped away.

Landi's mind spun all day, trying to find some way out of it. He thought of a hundred excuses by lunchtime and ran them all through his head standing in line at the pharmacy but none of them seemed to be good enough. As he tapped his foot on the floor, impatiently waiting to pick up his mother's pills, he happened to see a head of blonde hair a few isles away. His stomach fluttered. He began to sweat.

Is that her?

He tried not to stare but curiosity got the best of him as he eyed the blonde. With her back to him it was hard to tell anything. He hadn't seen her in three years; she could have looked completely different. Either way, he would know those sexy hips, full breasts and amazing thighs anywhere...

"Sir? Sir, can I help you?"

The pharmacist with oversized glasses looked annoyed as Landi quickly signed for the pills and waited.

It took forever for the medicine to be put into a small paper bag. Long enough to cause a panic attack. Landi kept one eye on the pharmacist, another on the blonde. He fidgeted, thought of more excuses, waited...

"Here you go. Have a nice day."

Landi took the bag and walked away from the counter when the blonde turned, causing his heart to jump.

Brown eyes.

He felt like a complete idiot, wanting to kick his own ass for getting so worked up over nothing.

As she often did, Jan had a sandwich already made up for Landi when he walked in the door. She smiled and gave him a kiss, taking the pharmacy bag.

"Thank you, sweetheart." Seeing her son looking a little distressed, she frowned. "What's wrong?"

"Nothing."

"You look uptight."

"I'm fine." He was actually relieved that no foreign cars were parked in front of the Coggwell's.

"Is it her?" Jan smiled, already knowing the answer.

"Who?"

"Dillan?"

"No."

"I saw her last night, went over to say Hi for a few minutes."

Landi raised an eyebrow, digging into his sandwich.

Mmmm. Egg salad.

"She's so beautiful, Landi. You have to see her, at least say hi. She's still the sweet, down to earth girl she always was."

"Well, I'm supposed to see her tonight…. Unless I can get out of it." *No! No! No!*

"You are? Have you talked to her?"

"No, I'm being forced into it."

Jan chuckled. "Good."

"Maybe everyone will finally get off of my back." *Yeah, great point.*

"Be nice to her." Jan warned.

He'd be nice, nice enough not to say anything.

All day at work Landi sent text message after text message to Jason explaining why he couldn't make it to dinner. Jason wasn't buying it. Landi knew he had to show up, at least for Jason. If he didn't, he could very well risk losing his best friend and that was not a risk he was willing to take.

I'll show up and duck out early. I don't even have to look at her.

♡

Landi had a strategy.

He left work and drove directly to Jason's, feeling much better with a plan in place.

Both cars sat in the driveway as he let himself in hearing music coming from the downstairs studio. He found Jason in the kitchen pouring a glass of water. This time he was in casual clothes. Much less intimidating.

"Hey, bro!" Jason smiled, happy to see his friend. "You come to try and get out of it?"

"No, but I'm going to need a few beers." *A few hundred.*

"Shall we go down to the old watering hole?"

"Hell, yeah."

"All right, let me go tell Tyann. I'll meet you at my car in a minute."

Landi nodded and headed for the front door with a slight smirk on his face.

Rude Awakening ♡

Tibby happily drank the last of her juice as she and Dillan pulled into the cobblestone driveway.

Dillan had promised Tyann she would stop by with Tibby before she had to take her back to her mother. The past few days had been nice getting settled and reacquainted. She had watched Tibby on Monday, took a break on Tuesday and had had her now since seven in the morning.

Hot, sweaty and exhausted from attempting to keep up with a two-year-old all day, Dillan struggled to get Tibby out of her car seat and onto her hip. She grabbed Tibby's juice as instructed, along with her purse and keys, shutting the car door with her flip flopped foot. Just as they reached the screen door, Tibby dropped her cup.

"Oh…Tibbs…" Dillan whined.

She anchored her keys between her teeth and squatted down to pick up the cup, wondering how she was going to open the door when the knob turned.

"Thank God…"

Relieved to have some help, Dillan stood....

And nearly pissed her pants.

Landi stood before her looking just as stunned as she was. Both of them speechless, she couldn't help but stare at him through the iron barred glass door. The keys fell from her mouth.

He was more filled out and slightly taller, looking a lot more like a man than the adolescent boy she used to know. She could see more definition in his muscles, a well-defined jaw and a hint of beard scruffle that was non-existent before. His hair was still long but more styled and kempt. And the laid-back grunge style that was his trademark lingered, only he seemed more put together and clean cut.

His sexy hazel eyes pierced through Dillan but something was different, very different. The sparkle that had once been in them was gone, replaced by a dark, hardened expression.

"I..."

"Hey Tibbs." His attention focused on the little girl.

She whined for Landi as Dillan set her down, fetching the keys.

Landi opened the screen door getting embraced by Tibbs.

What do I say? What do I do?

"Hey...Di..." Jason came to the door with a smile. "Ty's inside... she's downstairs."

"Thanks."

"We were just heading out but we'll see you later?"

"Yeah, okay." Dillan tried to catch Landi's eyes one more time but he wouldn't look at her. He completely ignored her.

Dillan's heart sank.

"Tyann!" She and Tibby ran downstairs and into the studio where Tyann was stretching in a hot pink tank top and yoga pants on the shiny wood floor. A myriad of colorful equipment lined the room: weights, rope, styrofoam shapes and large rubber balls. Hip-hop bounced off the walls at full volume.

"Tyann!" Dillan walked to the stereo, turned the music off and stood with her hands on her hips.

"Di! Tibbs!" Tyann smiled, and then frowned. "What's wrong?"

"Okay, first of all, look at me!"

"Yeeaah?"

Tibby giggled rolling around a big blue ball.

"I look like a big sweaty troll doll! I have food and apple juice all over me! My hair's all messed up! My face is all sweaty and greasy!"

"Di, calm down, you don't look that bad."

"No? I just ran into Landi, with Tibby on my hip and keys in my mouth. Oh God." She covered her face with her hands and fell onto a work out bench.

"What are you freaking out about, Di? He's seen you in every condition at one time or another, it's no big deal." Tyann went back to her leg stretch, unfazed.

"No big deal? I haven't seen him in *three years* and he sees me like *this*?" She tugged at her oversized men's t-shirt for effect.

Tyann bit her lip, trying not to laugh.

"So much for good second impressions."

"Well, you can make a good third impression at dinner."

"That's reassuring."

Dillan did feel a lot more confident all dolled up

wearing a sexy strappy top and her best jeans a few hours later. On her way up the drive for the second time that day, she saw the Toyota truck she had managed to miss earlier on the curb.

Her stomach fluttered.

Tyann walked out to greet her wearing a lacy cream blouse and black skinny jeans. A-maze-ing. Dillan made a mental note to copy the same look.

"It's okay Di, just relax and be yourself. He's still Landi, even if he doesn't act like it." The sincerity and genuine concern in Tyann's big brown eyes calmed Dillan's nerves. She was right.

He was still Landi…. right?

Tyann held her hand through the front door and into the living room. Dillan took one last deep breath before walking into the kitchen where Jason was cooking up a feast like a master chef. Vegetables were sizzling, steam was rising and smells were permeating.

And there was Landi.

He sat on a stool with a bottle of Coors watching Jason, his back to her.

"Hey Di." Jason looked up from his edible masterpiece.

"Hi." She sat one stool away from Landi and tried her best not to show how hurt she was that he was completely ignoring her… for the second time. Not that she was keeping count.

"You want a beer? Some wine?" Jason offered.

"A beer, please."

Look at me. Acknowledge my presence.

Landi's eye flinched in her direction for a split second, as if he'd heard her demanding thoughts. She couldn't believe how incredibly rude he was being and was tempted to knock him right off the stool just to get a reaction.

"What's the matter? You have something in your eye?" she heard herself say.

"Um…here, try one of these." Jason shoved a bowl of olives in front of her. She wanted to throw every one at Landi.

Tyann and Jason helped by starting some conversation but Dillan couldn't get over how weird it all was. He was acting like a completely different person.

Is this the same Landi? The one who loved me unconditionally? Who was my best friend? The Landi who knew me better than I did?

It didn't feel like it to her at all. He seemed cold, distant, hardened and very bitter.

The four had a good dinner despite the awkwardness but Dillan kept searching for a sign of the old Landi. She never found one. He left early not having said one word to her all night.

Just after his exit, Dillan sat on the couch with a glass of champagne deeply bothered by Landi's actions, or lack thereof. Tyann and Jason joined her sitting in a love seat across the way; hands interlocked like the high school sweethearts they were.

"So, what do you think?" Jason asked, obviously concerned. "He's changed hasn't he?"

Dillan stared mindlessly at the tiny bubbles in her glass. "I'm still trying to figure out if he's the same person I used to be with."

"Yeah, he's not the same old carefree Landi that he used to be," Tyann said. "There are times when the old Landi comes out though. I see it a lot when he and Jason are together."

"He hides it pretty well when he wants to, but it's there," Jason added.

"Is it me?" Dillan asked. "I mean, he didn't say one word to me. I got the impression he hates my guts."

"I think he's still angry, Di, aside from all of the other shit he's been through."

She knew he had been hurt. Besides her completely crushing him after high school, he'd had a string of bad relationships including a semi serious one that was going well until he was abandoned without any explanation. Dillan remembered when Tyann had called to tell her about it a couple years ago.

"Don't worry about it," Jason said. "He'll come around. Give him some time."

But all she could do was worry that night as she lay in the bed she and Landi had made love in too many times to count. She was feeling hurt and rejected, having lost the one person she thought would always be her friend.

♡

"So dinner was a bust?" Terry asked, taking a drink of her pink Cosmo.

"Big time. I think it's safe to say he doesn't want anything to do with me." Dillan hadn't been feeling like herself the past couple of days. She couldn't help but feel down after Wednesday night's dinner. The last thing she wanted to do was exactly what she was doing – clubbing on a Friday night. But Terry had been hell bent on taking her out and she couldn't refuse.

As she sat on a stool dressed to the nines sipping a Sex on the Beach, Dillan realized that it had been a while since she'd been a part of the nightlife. She found herself actually enjoying it. The energetic atmosphere, trendy music and artistic lighting were stimulating.

"It hurts, huh?" Terry asked, looking one hundred times more dramatic with dark, smoky eyes and defined lips.

"I just wanted to be friends again, that's all. Hell, I'd be happy if we were acquaintances."

"Do you still have feelings for him?"

"Yeah, I'll always have some kind of feelings for him, I can't help it." Dillan found herself wiggling to the music. "Do you think you'll ever get back together with Jesse?" she asked, wondering if she should have.

"I hope so. I keep telling myself we just need this little break and that everything's going to work out." Terry looked down at the table and crumpled up her cocktail napkin. "Sometimes I think I just need to move on, but it's not so easy."

"Hey, you gorgeous ladies want to dance?" Three adorable college guys surrounded them. Dillan couldn't help but be apprehensive. Her instincts told her not to take a chance – not to put herself in a scary situation with a stranger – but she ignored it, knowing it was only a wound from the past.

It didn't occur to Dillan just how drunk Terry had gotten until they were standing in front of Jesse's house – staring not only at his car, but the same Toyota that had been at Tyann and Jason's, along with Nick's and the 'mystery' car. Terry was blowing kisses at her ex's house. Dillan was trying to figure out why the hell she'd allowed Terry to navigate.

"Looks like they're having a guys night in," Terry slurred with a laugh.

"I knew I shouldn't have listened to you," Dillan mumbled, slipping behind a lilac bush. "Come on Terry, let's get out of here."

"Okay...I'm sorry...it's just that..." She burst into tears.

Dillan felt helpless and humiliated all at once.

"Come on, it's okay. Let's go talk at your house," Dillan hooked an arm around Terry's waist and spun her toward the car where the passenger door was still hanging wide open.

"I love you, Di. You always were such a good friend."

A good enough friend to let your drunken ass talk me into this mess.

Dillan practically shoved Terry into the car then quickly got into the driver's seat. A flick of light lit up the street. The motion detector on Jesse's garage spotlighted Landi and a pretty girl with long brown hair walking toward his truck. They were laughing and smiling – arms tightly and affectionately wound around each other.

"Shit!"

Dillan froze with shock, terror...and something else she couldn't quite grasp. Terry turned pale.

"I think I'm going to be sick." She reached for the door handle but Dillan stopped her.

"NO! Don't! He'll see us!"

"But..." Terry flailed her hands around, ready to upchuck at any minute.

Dillan kept a sharp eye on Landi and the girl as they hopped into his truck. She prayed they wouldn't drive by Terry's car.

"I have to...I can't hold it anymore!"

Dillan's lap was covered in vomit as Landi's truck sped away in the opposite direction.

Terry looked up at Dillan with big, teary eyes. "I'm

sorry."

Dillan awoke to a fruit loop being shoved into her ear.

Tibby was the culprit.

Dillan had crashed on Terry's couch after an exhausting night of water works; Terry crying her eyes out, while Dillan scrubbed away in the shower. The two had stayed up until three in the morning talking and laughing.

"Hey Tibbs." Dillan stole a hug from the little red head. "Where's your mommy?"

Tibby pointed to the front door, which was ajar. "Daddy," she said with a smile.

Dillan stood, getting a slight head rush, and crept to the door. Terry and Jesse were having an argument so she grabbed Tibby and twirled her to her room where they played with dolls and blocks.

"Hey Di."

She looked up to see a cute green-eyed Jesse smiling at her.

"Hi, Jess." She stood and gave him a hug, forgetting she was wearing nothing but a skimpy pair of girl boxers and white cotton tank top with no bra.

"It's been a while, huh? How are you? I heard you just got in not too long ago."

"I'm good. How about you?" Dillan's eyes wandered to his muscle shirt, defined biceps and trim build, then back to his eyes and stylishly messy brown hair. She always found Jesse attractive. Any girl with a pulse would.

"Ah, you know."

She smiled and nodded, not sure if she did.

"I hear you've been watching Tibbs, she seems to really like you."

"Yeah, we have lots of fun."

"I appreciate it."

Dillan smiled, not oblivious to Jesse's roving eyes. Apparently he shared the same attraction.

"Daaaa!" Tibby tugged on Jesse's leg, giving him puppy dog eyes to pick her up. He scooped her up and gave her a kiss.

"I'll see you around, huh?" Jesse said.

"Yeah, it's good to see you."

"You too."

Tyann: BBQ tonight. Bring drinks and your cute, sexy self. ;)

After yet another shower and a small nap in her own bed, Dillan was finally feeling refreshed and awake. She was actually looking forward to the get together at Tyann and Jason's that evening. It would be nice to see all of her friends together, even though she was leery about Landi and his girlfriend. Seeing them the night before bothered her, more than she wanted to admit. She'd never seen him with another girl. It was strange. She definitely wasn't looking forward to seeing them up close and personal but it was inevitable. She would deal with it and move on, no big deal. He probably wouldn't even look at her again.

Shoving her thoughts aside, she bounced downstairs to the smell of fresh baked goods to find her mom pulling out a batch of blueberry muffins from the oven. Dillan waited until the pan was resting safely on the stove before planting a kiss on her mother's cheek.

"Hey sweetie."

"Hi, mother dearest."

"Would you like a muffin?"

"Yes." She plucked one from its hole and sat at the table, gently peeling the paper away. "Where's Dad and Nick?"

Linda joined her daughter at the table with her own muffin, wiping away flour from her apron. "Your father's at the hardware store and Nick's with Erika."

"Do you like Erika?"

"I'm not so sure she's the one for him."

Dillan grinned. "You didn't answer my question."

"Yes I did." Her mother smirked right back. "She's a big partier and a bad influence on Nick."

Dillan nodded, diving further into her muffin.

"I'm going to walk over to Jan's in a few minutes and bring her some muffins." Linda stared blankly out the window. "You should come."

"I'd like to, but..." Dillan wasn't really sure what to say.

Would I piss him off going to see her? Would I be overstepping my boundaries?

"But what? She would love to see you. She's always talking about you, you know?"

"Oh?"

"Is it Landi?"

Dillan shrugged.

"What is with you two, anyway?"

"Nothing. He's mad at me or something. You should have seen him the other day – we had dinner at Tyann's and he didn't even say one word to me."

"I'll tell you what his problem is, he's still in love with you."

Dillan nearly spit blueberry muffin all over the table. "I don't think so."

"He's had a bug up his ass ever since you left this town."

The picture that came to Dillan's mind made her laugh so hard she was crying.

"Well? Are you going to come along or not?" Linda asked, amused that she had her daughter laughing so hard.

"Sure," Dillan managed. "If you insist."

Jan was ecstatic to see Dillan and Linda at her door. She excitedly gave each one of them a hug.

"Oh, my goodness! It's so good to see you, sweet Dillan."

Dillan felt the same; only she was saddened to see Jan looking frail and sickly. Her once thick dirty brown hair was thinning and she was much skinnier than she remembered.

Walking into Jan's home, Dillan was overwhelmed with sights and smells that brought her back – eerily so. The scent of Jan's essential oils and the Powell's signature laundry detergent invigorated her senses. Most of the furniture was exactly the same – never moved or replaced. Dillan was lost for words, taking it all in. How could she have stayed away so long?

"Dillan?" Linda grabbed her arm and took her to the patio where a pitcher of fresh lemonade sat in the middle of a four-person table. The muffins were a perfect addition.

The three sat outside in the shade of the umbrella, relaxing in the mid day heat.

"So, how are you doing, honey? You getting readjusted?" Jan asked Dillan who was still lost in thoughts from her younger days.

"Yeah, I had a good interview on Thursday and I have another this week. I'm going to start searching for a place to live soon."

"Not yet," Linda said, dramatically pushing out her lower lip.

"Well, I have to at least start looking."

"You can live with us for as long as you want."

"Mom, I'm not a little girl anymore."

"Yes, you are. You're my little girl."

Dillan rolled her eyes, trying not to laugh… or gag.

"Have you had a chance to see my boy yet?" Jan asked, already knowing the answer.

"Yeah, we had dinner at Tyann and Jason's on Wednesday," Dillan choked.

"How did it go?"

"Not so well."

Jan nodded but her gaze seemed far away. "Don't be fooled by his gruff exterior, he's still a kid at heart. Even now he has pictures of you in his old room; he kept everything you gave him. You were very special to him, you know? And you still are."

Dillan smiled, happy to hear such kind words, though she wasn't sure she could believe them. Landi's actions said something much different.

Dillan sat chatting with her mom and Jan until a nostalgic curiosity pulled her toward the house. After a couple glasses of tea, her bladder gave her the perfect excuse.

She walked to the bathroom, taking in the intoxicating aroma of the house all over again. She couldn't help but wander as the memories flowed. The living room and linen couch reminded her of the hundreds of times she and Landi had made out to movies; the kitchen of their silly cooking adventures and the guest room with the faux sheepskin rug where they'd made magical love. Then Dillan found herself drifting down the hall to Landi's old room. She stood in the doorway for a few minutes, just looking. It was almost exactly how she remembered it — except you could actually see the floor. His twin-sized bed was shoved in the corner with an Irish flag dangling above the headboard. The dresser was still just to the right of the window she'd crawled in about a million times. His dad's chest, littered with stickers, held a small television that she and Landi used to watch movies on. Jan kept the space clean, yet untouched. The mess was missing.

Dillan stepped in and took a deep breath as feelings and emotion overpowered her. Some part of her wished so much that she and Landi could be teenagers in love once again. All she wanted was to find a piece of the old him.

Without thinking, she walked to the closet and opened it to find old shirts of his still hanging. She grabbed a t-shirt she recognized and smiled, bringing it to her nose to inhale his smell. She was in a completely different world, feeling so close to that time, closer than she'd been in years.

Deadlock ♡

Feeling a slight hangover from the night before, Landi was not in the best of moods. He had stopped by his mom's for the day to help her out with anything that needed to be done and to see how she was feeling.

Walking into the house, he heard voices coming from the patio and looked to see his mom and Linda chatting away. He was glad to see his mom in good company and spirits. He was just about to join them when something caught his eye:

A third glass sitting by itself on the table and a chair halfway pulled out. His stomach churned.

He knew exactly whose it was, but where was she?

He walked to the hall, noticing the bathroom door was open, light off. A rise of anger hit him.

How dare she snoop.

Landi crept to his room and just about gasped at the sight.

Dillan stood before his old closet with a shirt

crumpled up in her hand, buried in her face. She looked so peaceful with her eyes closed cuddling the fabric as if it were…him?

He stared in shock, perplexed by her seemingly blissful moment. Did she still long for him and what they once had? Even after the distance and rejection he worked so hard at? His heart reacted at the thought, then something he hadn't seen in a long time caught his attention.

On her right index finger an orange stone set in white gold blinked at him. It was the promise ring he had given her years ago – that she apparently hadn't ever taken off. Mystified, he stood a minute then remembered he was mad.

"What are you doing?"

Her moment was immediately broken as she jumped and stared at him wide eyed. Wisps of blonde hair emerged from her messy ponytail. He almost wanted to laugh at the adorable sight.

She seemed to panic for a few seconds, lost for words. "Um…nothing. I was…just going… to the bathroom."

He opened his mouth to cuss her out but all that came out was, "Oh." He had completely lost all of his oomph staring into her sweet, beautiful eyes.

Without a word she simply walked around him, brushing his arm on the way out, leaving him with tingles he didn't acknowledge.

Landi watered flowers for his mother, picked out a few weeds, took out the trash and cleaned up the kitchen, all the while keeping a suspicious eye on Dillan. His mother called him out to talk or ask questions much more than she normally would, attempting to get him to sit with them. He couldn't help but notice the knowing grins she and Linda exchanged, amused by he and Dillan being within vicinity of each other. He just rolled his eyes and kept to his chores, minding his own business.

Once he was finished, he went out to say goodbye, not specifically directing it to anyone. He got a hug and a kiss on the cheek from his mother, a big smile from Linda and an unsure, half smile from Dillan, who still looked uneasy.

Relieved to leave the awkwardness behind, Landi got into his truck and sped away. The minute he turned off of Collister Drive his phone buzzed. It was Jesse.

Heading to gym in 30. Meet me there if you're up for it.

Beth's car was parked in the driveway. Landi wasn't sure whether to be grateful or apprehensive. One of Beth's downsides was a Jekyll and Hyde personality – he never knew what he was going to get. He couldn't read her...at all, which put him on edge more often than not. He chalked it up to her youth, though sometimes he questioned her state of mental health.

Once he saw the trail of clothes leading into the bathroom he knew what kind of mood she was in. No need for deciphering there. He peeked in on her soapy naked body, getting pulled halfway in.

"Hi, baby." She gave him a big wet kiss, tempting him to join her. His body responded immediately. "Get in."

"I want to but I'm meeting Jesse at the gym in a few."

She gave him pouty lips while running her hands over her perky breasts.

"Are you serving tonight?" he asked, keeping his eyes glued to her boobs.

49

"Yeah, Erika's hosting." Her expression turned serious. "What are you doing after the gym? Are you going to Tyann and Jason's?"

"Most likely."

"Is *she* going to be there?"

"Don't start." He withdrew himself from the show in the shower and shut the curtain.

"I just want to know."

Landi removed his shirt and fished his deodorant out of the medicine cabinet hoping to avoid conversation. Beth was the last person he wanted to relive ex-girlfriend memories with.

"Weren't you guys together for five years?"

"Six. Look, I don't want to talk about it. I have no idea if she's going to be there and I don't care."

Beth yanked the curtain back and peeked at him with wet doe eyes. "You know I'm not comfortable with it."

Landi sighed, went to the bedroom, slipped off his pants and found some clothes for the gym, then went back into the bathroom to deal with Beth.

"I don't know what to tell you, babe. I'm not going to stop hanging out with my friends just because she's there."

Silence made Landi wonder if he was going to get ripped.

"I just wish I could go with you," she said.

"You can come up after work, but I don't think I'm going to stay that long."

"Are you going to be here waiting for me?"

"You know it."

Beth peeked out at him with a cute grin. "Come here..." she purred. "Just for a few minutes. Let me give you a preview of what you're going to get tonight."

Landi wasted no time getting into the shower with his frisky girlfriend.

♡

Jesse was already bench-pressing when Landi got to the gym. No surprise. He never wasted time when it came to his own workouts since most of his days were spent helping other people work out. It was nice having a personal trainer as a friend.

Landi gave Jesse a surprise with a goofy face.

"What are you doing, you dork." Jesse set his weights down and sat up to laugh with his friend. "You're late, slacker."

"Yeah, sorry." Landi grinned.

"Oh, I see. You got a little pre-workout, huh?"

"Yep."

Jesse lay back down on the bench and readied to lift. "Spot me?"

The two did their usual weight routine then walked around the track a few times laughing and joking.

"What was up with Emily last night?" Landi asked. "She seemed kind of bummed or something."

Jesse glanced at the floor. His jovial mood disappeared. "She's been pushing me to get a divorce."

"Seriously?" The "D" word made Landi uneasy. "Holy shit."

"Yeah, I told her I'm not ready for that yet. I had no idea she was that serious, given the circumstances."

Jesse had been having an affair with Emily months before the separation with Terry. She knew all about Tibby and Terry long before the affair started but pursued him anyway.

51

"I was under the impression that this whole thing between us was just one big hot fling. I had no intention of it going any further. I mean, she's fucking smokin' and great in bed, but..."

"Not even close to being marriage material?"

"Exactly. And I love Terry, you know that. She's my wife."

"What are you going to do?" Landi asked.

"I don't know. I'm torn, as always." He took a long drink from his water bottle. "What about you?"

Landi's stomach lurched. "What about me?"

"You know what I'm talking about, man. I saw Dillan this morning – holy shit she's hot. How could you not be thinking about that?"

Landi shrugged. "I don't care."

"Yes, you do." Jesse smiled.

"No, I don't."

"Maybe you don't know it yet, but you do."

"You're wrong."

"Okay."

By the time Landi parked on the curb in front of Tyann and Jason's huge house, he was more than ready to relax and have a beer. The summer sun was beaming in the bright blue sky warming everything it touched. Scents of barbecues, fresh cut grass and flowers floated on the air. It was a perfect afternoon in the Briarhill neighborhood.

As Landi took in the surroundings, Jesse pulled up the drive. There was no way Landi was going to step in that house without him. Not with *her* lurking. She might corner him or try to smell his shirt... or both.

Jason and Nick greeted them wearing fluorescent surf shorts.

"Did I miss the memo?" Landi asked with a snicker. "I forgot my hot pink shorts."

"You're just jealous." Jason said with a smirk.

Landi watched as Jesse walked out the sliding glass door to the back patio where little Tibby was running around in a tiny bathing suit. Sounds of splashing and laughing came from the backyard. He noticed Tyann and Terry talking in some lawn chairs but no Dillan in sight.

"Hey." Her voice startled him. That voice. The unmistakable tone. She came up from behind him and joined the circle like one of the guys. Typical Dillan. He couldn't help but notice her not-so-masculine outfit – hip hugging shorts and a tiny tank top that accentuated her curves.

"Hey, sista!" Nick hooked his arm around Dillan's neck and held her in a playful deadlock.

"Stop!" She laughed. "Nick stop it!"

"Apologize for pushing me into the pool."

"No!"

"You're going to get it!" Nick swung her over his shoulder then ran outside to the pool with a squealing Dillan flailing to escape his grip. A scream and loud splash sounded. Landi smiled.

"You want a beer?" Jason asked with a smirk.

"Hell, yes."

Three beers later Landi was feeling amazing. Worries were gone, tension was melted and all was right with the world. All that mattered was enjoying time amongst friends. He didn't even care that much about Dillan's presence or the fact that his eyes kept spontaneously wandering in her direction. Except for the occasional accidental eye contact, he was doing pretty well avoiding her. Everyone was having a good time; even

Terry and Jesse were flirting a little whilst tending to their little one.

After the brats and burgers had been eaten, when the sun began to fade behind the hills, everyone migrated out to the pool. The air was thick with moisture, still warm from the midday heat. Crickets began to sing their nightly tunes.

Landi took a deep breath of balmy air encircling the pool before finding a lawn chair near the grass. Nick and Jason jumped into the turquoise water. Tyann sat on the edge of the hot tub with Terry and Jesse playing in the pool with Tibby.

Dillan wandered out with a smile but something was beneath it. Anxiety? Apprehension? Landi took a swig of beer. Why would she be uneasy amongst friends?

"Get in!" Nick yelled, splashing her.

Dillan began to undress. Landi looked away, not wanting to seem like he cared, even though he'd been dying to see what was underneath that tank top and shorts all afternoon. He pulled his own shirt off and sat back in the lawn chair, trying to focus on anything other than her.

Two seconds later he found himself staring at a body that caused every cell in his to stand at full attention. He was entranced, unable to do anything but gawk like a pervert. Her figure was incredible – toned, lean, curvaceous and much more womanly but the cute characteristics he had always loved were still there. The freckle on her hip, her slightly outie bellybutton, those little dimples above her butt...

"Hey!"

A splash of cool water jerked Landi out of his schoolboy trance.

"You okay, man?" Jason asked, grinning at him

from the pool.

Landi wiped the water from his face hoping nobody other than his best friend noticed how mesmerized he'd been.

"Yeah." He avoided looking in Dillan's direction desperately trying not to acknowledge how much she still affected him. He told himself he didn't like it, didn't care, it didn't matter anymore.

It wasn't until her back was to him that he noticed something he'd never seen before. A big scar, just on the left side of her lower back and another on her upper thigh. He frowned, positive it hadn't been there before. A new set of feelings emerged.

What the hell happened?

He felt sick. She'd been injured and he had no idea that it had even happened. He really had been wiped from her life. That thought made him feel even worse.

Landi sat paralyzed with worry and fear, unable to enjoy the beautiful evening and joviality going on around him. All he could think about was how lost he and Dillan had become. How far they'd grown apart. They were strangers.

He didn't want it to affect him so much…but it did.

Mixed Signals ♡

Dillan pulled up to Fitness Frenzy, exhausted from nearly finishing her second week of work. She was confident about her new position as a designer with FFC Interiors and even though she was beyond tired, she still made it a point to try and get to the gym a few times a week. It had nothing to do with the fact that Landi might be there.

The sun had just disappeared leaving a purple haze throughout the sky. Dillan took a minute to take in the cool summer breeze before click clacking through the front entrance in heels and business attire – black slacks, silk ruffle blouse, yellow cardigan and scarf; gym bag slung over one shoulder. She couldn't help but glance around as her card got scanned, wondering if Landi was there. They'd been running into each other everywhere the past week and a half, freakishly so. First it was coffee at a popular place, the grocery store late at night, then a gas station, home improvement store and the gym some nights after work. They never spoke, just looked at each other and went about their business. Awkward.

Sure enough, she noticed him sitting near the free

weights giving his muscles a rest between sets. She scanned his sexy body, remembering how incredible he looked without his shirt on at the barbecue. It was a vision she'd been enjoying the entire week. She always loved his lean lankiness but the manly muscles and slightly broader build got her womanly juices flowing. Something about him did amazing things to her.

Just as she was about to disappear into the women's locker room, they caught eyes. She quickly looked away and went in to change; wishing badly that she could just talk to him. But it was still way too soon. Wasn't it?

On the way home, Dillan stopped to get gas, more than ready to pour herself into bed.

She pulled up to the pump, got out and swiped her card then began the gas pumping, leaving the nozzle to wash her windows. As she smeared the windshield with solution, she glanced up to see a white truck a few pumps over.

Landi walked out of the small convenience store with a receipt in hand. Dillan's stomach flipped. He looked up at her. A smile slowly spread across his face.

"Are you following me?" he asked with a smirk.

"Believe it or not, no. I have better things to do with my time." She began to squeegee the water off of the window.

"I hear you have a new job? How's that going?"

"Good." She smiled at him, still completely shocked that he was actually speaking to her. "How's your mom?"

"She's alright. Hanging in there." He caught her eyes for more than a few seconds then looked away.

"I'm glad," Dillan said, trying to fill the silence.

"Well, I should go, but I'm sure I'll run into you somewhere."

"See you later." She watched him walk to his truck and get in, tickled that he had finally talked to her. Even though it was only a few words and a few minutes, it meant so much.

Once home, Dillan couldn't wait to take a steaming hot shower and fall into bed. She walked in the door finding the living room television on, but nobody was around that she could see...until Nick popped his head up from the couch.

"Hey sis, what's up?"

"I'm exhausted," she said, throwing her gym bag down.

Another head popped up from the couch. A girl she assumed was Erika.

"Hi." The girl scanned Dillan with skeptical eyes. Her dark makeup made her look evil.

Dillan went to the kitchen to get herself a glass of water as Nick and Erika followed. Dillan had to hold back a sigh of annoyance. She was not in the mood to meet new people.

"This is Erika," Nick said with a proud smile.

She was a petite, young-looking girl with dark brown hair.

"Nice to meet you." Dillan said, taking a drink of water.

"So, you're Landi's old fling?" she asked.

Dillan's stomach tightened. "Fling?"

"What do you do?"

"Interior design."

Erika looked at Dillan as if she were disgusting. "Oh."

Even though the guys wouldn't budge, it was obvious he was having an affair of some kind.

"I really think you should try and move on, Terry," Tyann said. "Screw Jesse. Let him do what he's going to do."

"I can't. I know things are going to work out, we just need more time."

"Even if he's screwing someone else?"

"He's not, and even if he is dating, or whatever, it's just a temporary, meaningless fling. He loves me and he *will* come back to me."

Dillan sighed. Potentially hurtful words were teetering on the edge of her tongue.

"How are you so sure?" Tyann asked.

"Because, he makes love to me at least once a week."

Tyann's eyes grew huge. "What?"

"Yeah, he crawls in bed with me and stays the night, sometimes just to snuggle, sometimes for more. But that tells me I'm still important and that things are looking up, right?"

"Umm.."

"Right." Dillan smiled, hoping she sounded reassuring. There was no way on earth she was going to deliver her opinion after that. "Hey, let's get out the yearbooks."

They dug through boxes and made a huge mess of Terry's living room but all of it was forgotten once they cracked open the memories. Dillan flipped to Landi's picture. She fell in love all over again with the sweet, long haired boy who'd stolen her heart. His wry boyish smile made her tingle.

"Remember how Landi hated Jesse when he first

61

met him?" Terry asked. "He thought Jesse was after you."

"Yeah, then they became best friends," Dillan said. "He was such a goofball."

Tyann grinned. "A goofball you loved. I miss you guys being together. Sometimes I wonder what it would be like now."

Tyann's words hit Dillan harder than she expected.

"I just want to be his friend right now, that's all. I want to get to know this new Landi before I even think about anything else."

Tyann handed Dillan a picture of her and Landi snuggled up together smiling, looking like the happiest kids in the world. They were around thirteen when everything was new and exciting. She missed those times.

"How did things get so messed up?" Dillan asked, feeling a wave of guilt. "Is it really all my fault?"

"No, Di. Things change, constantly." Tyann said. "You had to find yourself. If you stayed here everything would have been completely different – maybe not in a good way. I think the way things are now is how it's supposed to be." Tyann gave her a sweet smile, then a big hug. "I love you."

Dillan knew that Tyann felt her pain and loved her even more for it.

"Oh my God, look at my hair!" Terry said pointing to a freckled version of herself with pigtails.

They laughed the night away reliving good times, bad times and everything in between. Dillan did her best to enjoy her girl time but the nagging tug at her heart wouldn't go away. She longed for her goofy skater boy.

♡

"Mom, really? You're being silly. Please stop."

The minute Dillan stepped into the hardware store with her mother on that sunny Saturday morning she regretted it. Linda had decided to tell every worker and passerby that her daughter was the finest interior designer in town.

Dillan was flattered and embarrassed as hell.

"Okay, mom. Wow, check this out – you need one of these." Dillan whisked her mother over to the jacuzzis – a temporary distraction.

"Oooh, I think your dad would like that," Linda said, raising suggestive eyebrows.

"Ewe, yuck!"

Linda chuckled. "Okay, let's go over to the garden section. I want to pick out some flowers for Jan to pot."

And embarrass her some more.

As Dillan sifted through the plants, trying to find something she liked and camouflage herself via the foliage, a certain little voice caught her attention. She looked up to see Tibby, Jesse and an unknown female who looked like a model from the cover of a Seventeen magazine – his girlfriend. Dillan tried to control her rising anger.

Jesse and the girl were laughing and flirting with their hands all over each other as Tibby sat in the cart looking around for something to touch, or push, or pull. Her good eyes caught Dillan's and she smiled from ear to ear.

"Di, Di, Di!"

Jesse looked at Tibby and frowned, trying to figure out what she was saying.

"Di, Di!"

He finally noticed Dillan and a hint of guilt traced

his eyes.

Good.

They approached each other, breaking away from their companions.

"Hey Di, this is...awkward." Jesse said, nervously scratching the back of his neck.

"It's wrong is what it is. What the frick are you doing?" Dillan asked, placing her hands on her hips for effect.

"Emily's my girlfriend."

"That Terry has no clue about! She is hell bent over trying to get her family together while you're fooling around with Emily, behind her back, giving her mixed signals. I can't believe you, I can't believe you're putting Tibby in the middle of all of this."

"I know, I just...I need to find the right time to tell her. I don't want to hurt her."

"Too late."

Jesse looked to the floor like a cowering dog, then back up with eyes to match.

"You need to tell her, *now*," Dillan demanded.

"I know."

"Then *do it*, or I will."

"No, no, no...please, I'll do it. I need to tell her myself."

Dillan resisted the urge to punch Jesse. She marched past him and right up to Tibb. "Hey, sweetie."

Tibby reached for her and gave her a big hug. Dillan was delighted to see Tibby wearing the adorable nautical outfit she'd bought for her. She poked her in the tummy getting a giggle.

"How are you doing, cutie? I'm going to see you soon, okay?" Dillan glanced up at Miss Seventeen and shot her the best dirty look she could muster before going back to her mother.

Dillan broke away from her mother to call Terry. There was no way she could keep what she'd witnessed from her. It was time she knew the truth.

"Di?"

"Hey, Terry. I need to talk to you."

"What is it? Are you okay?"

"No, not really. I just saw Jesse… with a girl."

Silence. "Where? What girl?"

"This girl who looks really young."

"Oh, I think that's his friend, Emily. He's told me about her."

Dillan nearly dropped the phone. "What? No, they were flirting and everything."

"Jesse flirts with everyone. She's just a friend. I'm positive."

"Well, I'm not!" Frustration began to rise. "He told me she was his girlfriend!"

"Di, calm down. It's not a big deal, okay? He has a lot of *girl* friends and he calls them all his girlfriends. I'll ask him about it but I'm positive she's just a friend of his."

Dillan wanted to scream. Terry was so far in denial it was ridiculous. She ended the phone call furious at both Jesse and Terry.

Without thinking rationally she stomped back into the store and right up to Jesse.

"I don't know what the hell is wrong with you but you are an idiot!" she screamed, just before grabbing her mother's arm and storming out of there.

Dillan burst into tears on the car ride home causing Linda to pull over and hold her daughter tight.

"Sweetheart, what's the matter?"

Dillan wiped the snot from her nose and stared through blurry eyes at her mother.

"It's just not fair! All I want is to love and be loved – that's it! All of these idiots are running around cheating on each other causing all of this drama when people like me just want somebody. They don't realize what they have."

"Oh, honey." Linda reached for the tissue box in the back of her car and held it out for Dillan. "You will find your somebody. You will. Whatever is going on with your friends is their issue – not yours. Let it go. People choose to see what they want to see."

Dillan blew her nose, already feeling better letting her frustration out.

"You're a good friend, Dillan, and a wonderful person. I love how compassionate and caring you are but you can't fix everyone's problems. They have to work it out for themselves."

"I know," she said, defeated. "Ice cream?"

"Absolutely."

Dillan was exhausted by the time dinner was finished and was in dire need of fresh air. With a full stomach she decided to go for a walk down Collister Drive. She quickly learned that it was still one of her favorite things to do, knowing she would never get sick of the neighborhood and the flood of memories that came with it.

A gorgeous sunset laced with purple and pink clouds cast a haze of pastel throughout the sky. Smells of sweet grass and lilac were pungent on the air. Sprinklers coursed along lawns creating a stream along the curb. Dillan flirted with the mist, allowing the droplets to cool her every so often.

As she approached Jan's house on the way back,

Dillan saw Landi's truck parked in the driveway. She ignored it as best she could and went on her merry way, glancing just for a second toward the front door. She did a double take.

Landi sat on the front steps looking defeated. He stared down at the concrete, his body hunched and heavy.

Dillan's big heart swooned. She walked right up to the house and sat beside him on the step. They were silent. She heard birds chirping above.

"Are you okay?" Dillan asked, hoping she hadn't made a mistake.

"She's in a lot of pain today. I don't know what to do." He glanced up at her, catching her eyes for a split second.

It caused her stomach to quiver like Jell-O. She could feel his body heat seeping into hers causing even more internal reactions.

"I feel helpless," he said, looking back at the ground.

Dillan wasn't sure what to say, so they sat in a surprisingly comfortable silence. She enjoyed being so close to him as the light faded in the sky.

"Why did you move back, Di?" Landi asked, breaking the silence. His golden eyes pierced into hers.

"I was gone for too long. I needed to be close to my friends and family again."

"Why now?"

Dillan shrugged. "I don't know. Why?"

"I just don't get it." He fumbled with a loose string in the seam of his pants.

"What is there to get? I was tired of being so far away."

"Yeah, well...you could have decided that

sooner."

Dillan wasn't exactly sure what he meant, other than the fact that he still resented her for leaving him. She couldn't blame him.

"Where do you live?" Dillan asked, trying to keep things light.

"On the north end. I own that dark green house on Tenth Street."

Dillan smiled. "The one you always liked… and Beth lives with you?"

Landi suddenly looked uncomfortable. "Yeah, most of the time." He looked up at her. "What about you?"

"What do you mean? Isn't it obvious…I live with my parents, which is *so* much fun." She wasn't sure but it seemed like Landi's eyes lightened ever so slightly. He understood her sarcasm.

"Are you married, engaged?" he asked, annoyance lacing his tone. "You have a bunch of boyfriends strung about?"

"Nope." She smiled, happy that they were talking like friends.

"No? Are you sure?"

"Positive."

"How is that possible?"

She shrugged with a chuckle as Landi stood up and brushed off his pants.

"I should get back inside, see if there's anything I can do."

"Okay." Dillan stood and stepped down onto the grass. "Bye."

"See ya."

She could feel his eyes on her as she walked back to the sidewalk, delighted to have had her first conversation with him in years.

Tofu? ♡

Landi wasn't exactly sure when it had started but somehow, over the past couple weeks, he and Dillan had become acquaintances. He still kept his distance. It's not like they talked about anything important, they would just smile or wave when they ran into each other at the gym, or store, or wherever else it was that they saw each other. He was slowly starting to accept the fact that she was going to be around, which didn't bother him as much as he thought it would.

That particular weekend, Jason had informed him that everyone was helping Dillan move into her new townhouse – and that he should help too. Landi had heard the whole story from Nick about the move, how he was bummed about his sister moving out so soon, blah, blah, blah. Landi didn't care either way.

He called Jason on the way to his mom's neighborhood to make sure they were there, finally deciding to be a good sport and help out. Besides, if he didn't, he would never hear the end of it from his mom.

A storm blew in as he reached Collister Drive mixing rain and wind through the hot summer air. Landi was grateful for the change. Every one of his friends cars were parked along the Coggwell's home, some already loaded, some not. Landi grabbed a flannel from the backseat and crossed the street.

Jesse greeted him with a hand slap in the blowing rain. "What's up man?"

"Not much."

"I think we're about done loading, there wasn't much to do. She just had a few boxes."

"No furniture?"

"I guess she's buying new stuff?" Jesse shrugged.

"I'll run up and see if there's anything I can do."

On the way in the house he passed by Terry and Tyann. A clap of thunder boomed as he walked in seeing Nick and Mrs. Coggwell who gave him a kiss on the cheek and a cookie. He scarfed the chocolate chip treat on his way up the stairs and ran into Jason at the top.

"Hey man!"

"Hey, what's going on?" Landi asked.

"Di's just getting the last box, then we're headed over to the new place. Is it raining?"

"Yeah, just started."

"Damn, I better make sure everything's covered."

Jason ran downstairs as Landi stood, hesitating. He wasn't sure if he should follow Jason or go into the room he hadn't seen in years. Something pulled him to the pink room. He found himself standing just inside the doorway, looking around in awe, taking it all in. It looked *exactly* the same as it had when he was younger. He now understood why Dillan had wandered into his old room a few weeks ago.

71

"It's weird, isn't it?" A voice from below asked.

He glanced down to see Dillan sitting on the floor taping up a small box. Her hair was in a messy knot atop her head, blonde locks hung in her eyes and a few black smudges stained her face. To top off the look she was wearing an oversized t-shirt and small shorts. She looked adorable.

"Yeah, it really takes me back," he said, losing his thoughts momentarily.

He scanned the room again seeing pictures of himself still tacked to the wall. Something inside of him numbed. He instantly put his guard up, not wanting to see or feel any of it anymore.

"Thanks for coming over." She stood with the box in her hands and held it out to him. "This one's for you."

His stomach tightened. "What is it?"

"For you to carry...so this isn't a complete waste of your time."

"Oh, right." He took the box, feeling slightly embarrassed.

Just for a second they locked eyes. It was as if the world disappeared and time had never gone by. The two of them alone in her room where they always were – where they were meant to be. A vortex of Dillan and Landi. Thunder cracked, intensifying the moment.

Linda appeared in the doorway. "Oh, sorry..." With eyes wide she turned and walked away. Dillan laughed and then left the room as he lingered, just for a couple more minutes.

Dillan's new townhouse was just a few blocks away from the famous Collister Drive in a beautiful neighborhood amongst old homes. It was brick on the outside and spacious on the inside, clean, bright, and homey – perfect for one person.

This isn't how it was supposed to be.

Dillan was beaming as everyone helped carry in the boxes in the dying rain as the storm blew over. The sight of Dillan's belongings caused a crater in his chest. He tried to ignore the feelings stirring in him but they wouldn't go away.

When the furniture and boxes were settled, Dillan ordered pizza for everyone. They all gathered in a circle on the floor to talk. Landi went out to the small balcony in the living room overlooking a green landscaped yard. He didn't want to stay much longer, feeling out of place.

"It's nice, huh?" Jason asked, leaning on the railing.

Landi didn't even bother making eye contact. "It's not bad."

"What's up, man? You seem kind of bummed. Is this weird for you?"

"I'm fine. I've got to get to my mom's and do some things at home."

Jason shot him a piercing look. "You're not going to stay?"

He shook his head.

"Why not, dude? You're amongst friends, we just ordered food – why don't you have a beer and chill out?"

"Because I don't want to."

Jason sighed with irritation. "Come on, Landi. You're being a dick. Suck it up and deal. I know Di would appreciate it if you stayed."

Silence filled the air as all of the tension broke loose. Something inside Landi snapped.

"I don't give a shit what she appreciates," he yelled. "I'm out of here."

He left without saying goodbye to anyone, feeling distant from everyone, including himself.

♡

Mid-week, Landi was still feeling like an ass for leaving Di's new townhome the way he had. He wasn't sure what had come over him. He'd made a point to apologize to everyone...except Dillan. He had much bigger plans in mind for her. His idea was to invite her over for dinner at his house to make up for him skipping out on the pizza.

The problem was he couldn't muster up the nerve to do it.

He didn't want her getting the wrong impression, didn't want her to think they were suddenly BFF's or dating again. He just wanted to do something nice, that was all, without making a big deal out of it. Maybe get to know her again a little better, nothing else. The other problem was Beth. He knew she would flip having Dillan anywhere near the house, even if she wasn't there, but that was second on his worry list. It was his house; he could do whatever he wanted.

On Thursday evening, Landi skipped the gym and headed for the grocery store. He had circled most of the store and was just about done when she caught his eye.

Nice ass.

Still in her girly gym clothes, Dillan held the same red plastic basket that Landi did in one hand, a package of something he'd never seen in the other. She carefully examined it, lost in contemplation as he inspected the items in her basket: a couple of potatoes, a half-gallon of milk, some spices.

It hit him – he would invite her over right then.

74

With more than enough of what he needed already at home and in his basket and Beth at Erika's for the night, it was perfect.

He walked up from behind her with a grin. The smell of her hair was intoxicating. "What is that?"

She turned to look at him with startled expression. "Landi…hi, it's tofu."

"Tofu?"

"Yeah." She gave him a playful smile – the one he adored.

"What happened to the meat and potatoes girl?"

She laughed. "I've got the potatoes." She held up the basket making him laugh. "I was just trying a new recipe for dinner, with the tofu."

"Okay, you're coming home with me."

She chuckled. "What?"

"I can't let you eat that, I'm sorry."

She peered at him, squinting ever so slightly.

"Plus, I was kind of a jerk the other day for bailing on you and not saying goodbye, so I'll make you dinner… to make up for it."

Dillan looked up at him with her big, green eyes. He'd won this battle. "All right, I guess I can skip the tofu."

An hour and a half after the grocery store meeting there was a knock on Landi's front door. He left the kitchen where he had already started dinner and opened the door to see Dillan looking cute and casual in a tight pair of jeans, sexy pink top and hair in a high ponytail.

"Welcome," he said, stepping aside for her.

"Thank you." Dillan smiled and slowly walked into the room, gripping her purse.

He could sense her unease. "Make yourself at home. Take your shoes off. Whatever you need to do."

"Wow, I'm impressed," she said, looking around at his bachelor pad.

He raised an eyebrow.

"It's clean."

"Yeah?"

"I wasn't aware that you were capable of keeping a clean space." She grinned, teasing him. "You have to admit, your room was a black hole."

He smiled, knowing she was right. "Okay, I admit it."

Dillan set her purse down on the coffee table and followed him to the kitchen where he got her a beer before checking on the salmon in the oven.

"Mmmm, it smells amazing," she said, closing her eyes to savor the scent. "Seriously. Where did you learn to cook?"

"Jason. He dragged me into his little cooking world."

"Really? I would have never pinned you as the cooking type," she said, leaning on the counter to watch him do his thing.

"Me either," he admitted. "Surprise!"

He got a chuckle out of her, which made him smile.

He allowed Dillan to carry his beer for him but nothing else. This meal was for her and he was determined to let her know it. They sat at his small four-person dining table and talked about jobs and other mild topics. Landi was enjoying himself and was pleased with how everything turned out. Dillan's exaggerated "Mmm's" and "Wow's" let him know he'd succeeded at impressing her. Her enthusiasm at the dinner table was a reminder of how passionate she was – in the bedroom and otherwise.

Landi had to force himself to think about anything other than her passion.

After eating, they sat in the living room opposite each other, drinking beer from bottles. Landi lounged on his brown leather couch while Dillan sank into it's matching loveseat. Landi's eyes wandered over her body.

"That was great, thank you," Dillan said, wedging her beer between her thighs. She rested her feet on the edge of the coffee table.

"You're welcome."

She smirked at him. "I have to admit, I was a little worried."

"Why?"

"When we were young, you could make a disaster out of a peanut butter and jelly sandwich."

"No way." He teased.

"Admit it."

"No."

They laughed until silence engulfed the room. It was finally beginning to feel like they were friends again.

Landi took a swig from his beer noticing Dillan's mood grow serious. When she looked up at him with pensive eyes, he knew he was in for an awkward conversation.

"How are you? Really?" She asked, piercing him with a look that made him uncomfortable.

He avoided her gaze. "Fine."

She sighed, unsatisfied with his answer. "Are you happy?"

"What do you mean?"

"I just want to know if you're happy."

He shrugged, not at all wanting to talk about his happiness, or lack thereof.

"Are *you*?" he asked, turning the tables.

"In my own way, I suppose."

Landi took a long drink of beer then leaned back into the couch, closing his eyes to avoid any more talk.

"You've changed a lot."

His eyes shot open as he sat up, ready to defend himself. "What did you expect?"

"I don't know." She looked down at the floor in discomfort.

A part of him felt guilty. "So tell me the real reason why you're single, what's the deal?"

"I guess I'm too picky and stubborn."

He nodded. "I can see that."

She jokingly squinted her eyes at him, and then smiled.

"That's it?"

"Pretty much. I never stayed in one place very long so..."

"But surely you've dated off and on?" He pushed.

"Well, yeah. But either I leave or they leave me."

Landi frowned, puzzled. What man in his right mind would leave her? "Why would anyone leave you?"

She looked lost in thought and hesitation. "I don't give them what they want."

"Marriage," he said matter of factly. He had been in that boat.

"No."

"No?" Now he was truly baffled.

She sighed and took a sip of her beer as if to try and end the conversation. She had poked and prodded him, now it was her turn.

He gave her a look to go on, waiting for her to

speak up. Finally she rolled her eyes and sighed again as Landi took a drink.

"If you must know, I don't sleep with them."

Landi spewed beer in every direction, then attempted to gather himself whilst wiping away beer foam from the couch with a dirty t-shirt.

Dillan was practically rolling with laughter.

"You're joking right?"

"No."

He laughed even harder, not believing it. "You're telling me that..." He paused, trying to soak it all in. "You've never slept with *any* of the guys you've dated in three years?"

"No." She shook her head, looking serious now.

"Are you a lesbian?"

She chuckled. "I've thought about it but no."

Landi waited. Waited for her to tell him that the joke was up. He kept waiting but she looked dead serious.

"Why?"

She shrugged, obviously not wanting to talk about it. Had something happened to her? He suddenly panicked inside.

"Is everything okay?"

"Yes." Her face flushed and he felt bad for embarrassing her.

The wheels turned as they sat in silence. Why wouldn't she sleep with anyone? Was it because of him? Of them? What they had? Did she still have feelings for him? Had she just not found the right guy? It didn't make any sense. Did something happen, something terrible that scarred her for life? He suddenly remembered the scars and his stomach dropped.

He had to know the truth.

Fireworks ♡

Ninety-seven degrees.

That's how hot it was the day of the Fourth of July barbecue at Tyann and Jason's the following weekend.

The temperature had nearly hit one hundred within the past few days leaving everyone hot, miserable and sticky. Dillan was glad for the "cool down" as she and Tyann hung festive decorations all around the pool, throughout the backyard and inside where Jason was setting up the food.

Dillan couldn't help but smile thinking about the dinner she had with Landi Thursday night. She felt as though they were slowly becoming friends again and it meant so much to her. She was looking forward to seeing him again that evening, knowing things would be even better between them.

Nick and Erika arrived early and before anyone else showed up, Dillan slipped away to the upstairs bathroom to change into a flattering short summer dress with her bikini underneath. She tied her hair up into a messy but cute knot and powdered her face, then happily bounced down the stairs, ready for the evening.

To her surprise about seven people who she didn't recognize had arrived while she was changing. She mingled a little, introducing herself to Iyann and Jason's friends and coworkers when Landi and Beth caught her eye. They had obviously just arrived and were still being greeted outside by the pool as Dillan watched intently through the sliding glass door from the living room.

Stupid! Stupid! Stupid! How could you forget about Beth?

Beth clung to Landi like a lost child – meek, shy and naive. Dillan carefully scrutinized her, not wanting to miss any details. She was thin in an annoyingly attractive way like a high fashion model. She had long wavy hair clinging perfectly around her twenty year old body. Gag. Her style was bohemian all the way – that hippy-ish, wild style that seemed effortless. She was definitely a natural beauty.

Dillan's stomach tightened as she watched them interact. She saw right away that they were comfortable with each other, but not in love.

Dillan tried to kill her nerves with a deep breath. Anxious butterflies wracked her stomach. She plastered on a convincing smile and approached them, noticing Beth was even prettier up close.

"Hi." Dillan smiled, knowing she was exuding confidence.

Landi looked uncomfortable, obviously not prepared for the sudden introduction, so Dillan went ahead and did it herself.

"I'm Dillan, you must be Beth?"

Beth stiffened as if she had just found out Dillan

was contagious with something.

"Yeah." Instead of smiling Beth's face was blank and cold. She held onto Landi even tighter as if to say, 'he's mine'.

Dillan got the hint. "It's nice to finally meet you," she said with the biggest, most sincerest smile she could muster. "I'm sure we'll be great friends."

How much further could she push?

"I heard you go to BSU. Did you just graduate from high school?" Dillan asked.

Landi widened his eyes and tilted his head ever so slightly. She was being warned.

"We're going to go grab a drink," Landi growled.

"Okay, I'll see you guys around."

Another deep breath later Dillan found herself in the kitchen getting…

A bottle of vodka. She took a swig before Tyann came up from behind her and yanked it away.

"What the hell are you doing, girl? Jesus!" Tyann set the bottle down and proceeded to make her a real drink – the kind that go in fancy glasses.   Dillan couldn't believe her friend was walking around the house in nothing but a pink bikini. Actually, she could. She wiped the sweat from her brow and sighed. "I assume you met Beth. What do you think?"

"Well, she seems to hate my guts, that's pretty normal for a girlfriend."

"They just don't go together." Tyann's pink hammocked boobs jiggled when she set a yellow concoction in front of her.

Dillan shrugged and took a few sips.

"Don't even act like you don't care."

"What?" She smirked, already feeling dizzy.

"I saw you watching them."

"So?"

"Is it weird? I can't imagine seeing Jason with another girl, even if it was three years later."

"No, we're past that." Truthfully, she wasn't so sure she was. It did hurt; she just didn't realize it until that moment.

Once Terry and Tibby got there Dillan relaxed even more. She was feeling self-conscious and a little out of place, staying as far away from Landi and Beth as possible. Tibby wanted Dillan to hold her constantly so she was entertained by the little girl until it began to get dark.

Everybody ate and drank; waiting for the fireworks in the hot summer air as Dillan hopelessly found herself watching Landi and Beth in the twilight. She watched him touch her, kiss her, tend to her like a loyal companion. Every smile, laugh, gesture between them seemed to tug at her heart and before she knew it she was drowning the pain away with way too much alcohol.

Just before the fireworks started, Jesse arrived, giving Terry and Dillan a much needed break. Terry tried to get Dillan to be silly with her, being all overly dramatic with the 'oohs' and 'aws' but all Dillan could think about was Landi and Beth. It didn't help that they stood in clear sight beneath the white decorative lights, Beth laughing and tossing her hair, giving him kisses with her hands all over him. Dillan wondered if she always acted like that or if she was playing it up. Either way it was annoying.

When the fireworks were over, Dillan was just about to get herself some more alcohol when Tyann dragged her inside and into a spare bedroom.

"Are you okay?"

"I'm fine," Dillan said, dizzy and on the verge of

tears.

"No, you're not. You've had a lot to drink. No more."

"Is Beth always so…animated?"

Tyann laughed. "I don't know, I don't really pay much attention. She's usually quiet and keeps to herself most of the time unless Erika is around."

That didn't make Dillan feel any better. "She's hanging all over him. And those damned lights make it look so dreamy and romantic…"

"Di, stop. You're overthinking it. I guarantee Beth is playing it up since you're here."

She looked into Tyann's deep dark eyes and lost it, bursting into a frenzy of tears.

"I hate her! She's so perfect and thin…give me an f'n break! Who acts like that? Who actually laughs and giggles like a…middle schooler? Like she even gives a real shit about him…"

"Okay, it's alright."

"I just can't stand it, Ty…It hurts…it hurts so bad…" Dillan wailed, unable to control her tears or her mouth. The pain was eating at her.

Tyann wrapped herself around Dillan, happy to let her best friend cry on her shoulder. "It's okay, Di. It's okay to be sad."

Dillan tried desperately to get herself together sniffling and gasping for air. She fell onto the bed and cried into the pillow.

"I'm going to go get you some coffee, okay? Stay here." Tyann disappeared as Dillan closed her eyes and drifted until a bounce on the bed woke her.

"Dillan? Are you okay?"

Terry sat looking at her with a worried expression.

"No."

"Oh, honey." Terry lay beside her and gently rubbed her arm. Dillan was grateful for the comfort and friendship, even if Terry was completely delusional.

"Where's Tibbs?"

"Her grandma came to pick her up. This party is getting a little too wild for my child."

They laughed at the ridiculous rhyme.

"Have you talked with Jesse, yet? About his girlfriend?"

Terry looked away. "No, but things are better between us and I don't want to mess things up with any more unnecessary drama."

Tyann appeared with a mug of coffee and joined them on the bed.

"Do you just want to crash here?" she asked. "You're not missing much."

"Yeah, I think I'm done… but I have to go pee."

"I'll go with you," Terry said, helping her up and off of the bed.

Surprisingly, Terry made Dillan feel better with a silly bathroom break. They powdered their noses, put on a little eye makeup, confettied themselves with shimmer, downed coffee and giggled like teenagers. Dillan forgot all about her Landi woes until she walked back out into the hallway.

Erika and Beth were standing in the living room laughing and giggling in their own world. The minute Beth noticed Dillan she snickered and whispered to Erika.

Dillan wanted to smash her ugly face. Caffeine and adrenaline had her wide-awake.

"What the hell is that?" Terry's question distracted Dillan from her evil thought. She turned to see Terry staring at Jesse as if he had three heads. Terry's face turned three shades of red.

"Terr? Terry?" Dillan looked at Jesse, trying to find something, anything... but he looked like the same old Jesse with just one head.

Terry marched straight up to Jesse who looked terrified.

"I need to talk to you, NOW!"

The huge living room seemed to fall silent. Even Landi and Jason who were still outside poked their heads in to see what was happening.

Dillan watched as Jesse and Terry disappeared into the bathroom, wondering what had come over Terry so suddenly. After only a couple of minutes there was yelling coming from behind the bathroom door.

Tyann walked over to Dillan who was standing bewildered between the hallway and living room.

"What's going on?" she asked.

"I have no idea."

Terry stormed out with tears streaming down her face looking like she was on a mission. She walked straight out the back door with Jesse at her heels, obviously upset.

Dillan was worried about her friend. "I'm going to go see what's going on."

"I'm with you."

They ran around the house in the dark past the pristine landscaping toward the front. Dillan tripped on a solar light.

"Owe! Fuck!"

"Di, are you okay? Where are you?" Tyann asked.

"I impaled myself on a stupid light." Dillan felt a sharp pain in her ankle but got up and limped toward

Tyann where yelling was coming from the front of the house. Terry and Jesse were having a full-blown argument in the driveway. Lights from the house and landscaping lit up the yard like a movie set. How appropriate.

"...You stupid inconsiderate prick!" Terry screamed. "How could you do this to me? To us?"

"I didn't..."

"I knew you were fucking someone else! I knew it! Did you think I wouldn't find out? Do you think I'm stupid?"

"No! Would you shut up for two seconds so I can explain?"

Landi, Jason and Nick came out through the front door looking ready to get involved if need be. Dillan wondered if they even noticed her and Tyann in the shadows.

"Explain what, Jesse? Why you threw your family away for a fucking slut!"

Terry walked to Jesse's brand new car on the curb and swiped at its side panels. A metallic screeching sound filled the air.

"What the fuck are you doing?" Jesse yelled, running toward her with his head in his hands.

"Don't worry, this won't hurt as much as the divorce is going to!"

"Stop it! Terry, stop it! God dammit!" He grabbed her from behind and physically pulled her away causing Dillan to lose it. Old scars surfaced bringing anxiety, fear and uncontrollable adrenaline. She ran toward Terry, ready to protect her friend at any cost.

"Jesse, STOP!" She yelled. "Let go of her!"

At Dillan's words he released her, getting punched square in the nose by Terry's fist. That's when Dillan noticed the hickey on Jesse's neck – the fire starter.

Terry ran to her car in hysterics. Dillan followed and climbed into the passenger seat, barely shutting the door before Terry sped off.

"Terry, please slow down, you're scaring me."

"That stupid piece of shit! I knew it! I knew it, Di." She ripped around the corner causing Dillan's body to slam against the car door.

"Terry, slow down!" She yelled.

"I'm going to find her and I'm going to kill her! I'm going to make him suffer for this, both of them! He can kiss his daughter goodbye!" She began crying uncontrollably.

"Terry, please pull over." Dillan begged. "You're in no condition to drive. We're going to get pulled over!"

"Is that him behind me?"

Dillan looked to see a car following closely behind.

Please don't be the cops. Please, oh please, oh please.

"Pull the fuck over, Terry! We're going to get arrested! Neither one of us should be in a vehicle right now."

"I'm sorry," Terry cried. "You're right."

Dillan reached for the steering wheel. She was jerked around as if on a rollercoaster ride. Out of control. Confused. The cab began to spin. Darkness enshrouded them. Sounds of the blinker registered, along with moaning and a blaring horn. Dillan's head was throbbing with pain. She knew they were no longer moving, though she wasn't sure what direction she was in. Dizziness kept her veiled in confusion.

"Di? Di?" Terry's shaky voice. "Di, look at me. Can you look at me?"

Dillan moved her head in the direction of the voice

seeing a blurry Terry wide-eyed and frantic.

"Oh God, you're bleeding!"

Dillan put a hand to her head feeling warm blood. Terror ripped through her body.

Not again.

She couldn't breathe. Tears formed. Then he appeared. Her sweet prince.

"Di? Di? Are you okay?" He asked, looking just as terrified as she felt.

She didn't know how to answer.

No, rescue me, my love.

Suddenly Landi was in her face asking her questions, checking her head, neck…body.

Did I put deodorant on?

"Don't move, okay?"

Dillan admired Landi's sweet, caring eyes and how close he was, kneeling at her side with her hand in his. He took his shirt off and held it to her head.

"Is this a dream?" Dillan asked.

As if it were too much to handle, Landi lowered his head. The last thing Dillan remembered seeing were tears rolling down his cheeks.

Spending the latter half of the evening in the emergency room with a mild concussion was not exactly what Dillan had in mind for the Fourth of July. Terry had hit a streetlight at around thirty-five miles an hour, damaging her car and Dillan's head. Terry had walked away with no injuries having had her seat belt on out of habit, even after all the craziness. Dillan hadn't had time, hence the head injury. The right side of her head got a beating with a small, deep cut and her chest was a little bruised, but luckily that was it. Besides being a little shook up, hazy and dizzy, she was feeling okay.

Landi, Nick and Jesse had followed Dillan and Terry in Jesse's car until the accident. An ambulance, fire truck, police car and tow truck had all arrived on the scene, though Dillan had thankfully blacked out during all of that drama. She was now lying awkwardly and uncomfortably on a cot in a small intake room waiting for stitches and the doctor as friends drifted in and out.

Terry wept by her side feeling terrible about everything. Dillan had tried to calm her but it wasn't working. Terry was completely distressed about the whole evening.

Nick came back from the bathroom looking exhausted. Dillan widened her eyes at him ever so slightly to try and give him a clue that Terry was driving her nuts and increasing her head pain.

"Hey…did the doctor come back yet?" he asked.

Dillan lightly shook her head, not wanting to make her headache worse.

"All right, I'm going to go with Jesse back to Tyann and Jason's to pick up my car so I can drive us home. Why don't you come with me, Terr?"

"No, I want to stay with Di. It's the least I can do," she managed.

"Honey, you need some sleep. Don't worry about me, I'll be fine. Besides, you're going to need to be functional for your daughter tomorrow."

"I'm going to be with Di all night." Nick assured her. "I'll make sure she's okay."

Terry gave Dillan a big hug, clinging to her a little too long.

"I'm sorry, Di. I'm so sorry."

This time Nick had wide eyes as he pried Terry from Dillan and rushed her out the door.

"You going to be okay alone for a while?" Nick asked.

"I think I'm in good hands."

He smiled at her before disappearing.

Minutes felt like hours as Dillan waited on her cot. *It's a good thing I'm not bleeding to death; I'd be dead by now.* She chuckled to herself when Landi walked in, surprising her. He looked tired... and handsome as hell. His t-shirt was stained with what she presumed was her blood. His arms were dirty, he was scraggly and worn down but damn he was sexy. He pulled off the grungy look a little too well.

"Do you mind if I sit with you for a few?" he asked.

"No, not at all."

Dillan watched as he sat in a plastic visitor's chair and rubbed his eyes.

"So what's going on?"

"I'm still waiting for results," she said. "Did my brother leave?"

"Yeah, they all left."

He stayed just for me.

Her stomach fluttered. "Thanks for sticking around."

"I'm just glad you're okay."

They looked into each other's eyes for a couple seconds until the doctor finally walked back in. According to him the test results were good but he still gave her precautions. As he was speaking his pager went off and he was gone again.

"Jesus, these emergency rooms are always so hectic," Landi said. "You're lucky if you get to talk to the doctors for five minutes."

Dillan shrugged.

"It's exactly the same when I come with my mom." He sat back in the chair. "One minute they're here, the next they're gone, and you never know when they'll be back. We could be here all night."

We.

Dillan wanted so much to ask about Jan but she wasn't sure if she should. She contemplated it for a few minutes, trying to read Landi. She didn't want him leaving her, she was enjoying his company.

"All right, Dillan, sorry about the wait..." The doctor appeared frowning at his clipboard. "It says here that you've had an allergic reaction to stitches? From severe lacerations you had a few years ago? Is that right?"

Her stomach sunk. She was suddenly nauseous.

"Um, yeah." She could feel her face flush. She wanted more than anything to crawl under the hospital bed she was sitting on.

"So we'll use steri-strips this time for your head..." He kept blabbing on about the strips and the procedure but all Dillan could think about was the look on Landi's face. She could see it well out of the corner of her eye. He was curious and concerned. She wanted to hide her secret forever, never talk about it again, especially with him.

He couldn't know the truth.

As soon as the doctor left, Dillan knew what was coming. She was prepared.

"What happened?" he asked, stone serious.

"Surfing accident."

He nodded, not looking convinced. Dillan found the dirt on his chin charming.

"I fell into some sharp rocks, it was stupid, really."

"I never heard about that."

She shrugged. "It wasn't a big deal."

"Sounds like it was."

"Well, yeah…I mean, it sucked for sure."

"Is that what those scars are from?"

The scars. Shit!

"Yeah."

"Tell me about it."

"Okay…"

Thankfully a nurse saved her ass… and her head. Dillan was temporarily relieved, knowing that wasn't the end of it.

They'd just finished applying the steri strips when Nick arrived with a worried sick Tyann. She coddled Dillan like a baby, staying close to her side while Nick and Landi entertained each other in the guest chairs.

At three in the morning, Dillan was finally released. They all piled into the car and headed to her townhome.

The first thing she did was crawl into bed – not caring about anything other than rest. It felt even better than she had imagined as she closed her eyes and sank into the mattress.

"Hey, you."

She looked up to see Landi's beautiful hazel eyes. She wanted more than anything to pull him into bed with her for a snuggle.

"I'm heading out. Nick's going to drive me up the hill."

"Okay, thank you…for everything."

"Where's your phone?" he asked.

"My wha…?"

"Right here." Tyann chimed, conveniently holding it out to Landi. He grabbed it and began typing on the screen.

"What are you doing?"

"I'm entering my number so you can call me and tell me how you're doing."

"Oh..."

Tyann smirked over Landi's shoulder, and then gave her a thumbs up. Dillan laughed.

"Are you a little loopy?" Landi asked, still concentrating on his phone number mission. He set the phone on her nightstand. "Call me tomorrow, er, later today, okay?"

"Okay." She smiled and watched him leave, then fell fast asleep.

Having two people wake you to pester you with questions every hour doesn't make for good sleep. Dillan awoke feeling groggy, tired, dizzy and hung-over.

Nick left around noon while Tyann and Dillan lounged in her bed discussing the insane night. Dillan was happy to be warm and snuggled in her home with her best friend. Besides her aching head, it was a perfect morning.

"I can't believe Jesse, what an ass!" Dillan vented. "He could have had the decency to not show up with that enormous hickey."

Tyann laughed into her pillow then faced Dillan. "He didn't know he had it. According to Jason he had a romp with his girlfriend just before showing, which was why he was late and she accidentally sucked too hard."

Dillan rolled her eyes making Tyann chuckle again. "Everything is like a huge blur, it seemed so intense and crazy at the moment but I hardly remember anything."

"I know, I still can't believe Terry got you guys into an accident."

"She was so upset."

"At least she knows about Jesse's stupid girlfriend

now."

"Oh my God, don't even get me started." Dillan grumbled. "I could have wrung her neck too for not believing me."

There was a pause as the friends processed everything in silence. Dillan closed her eyes for a moment thinking of Landi.

"What happened to Beth and Erika once everyone left?" she asked.

"They hung out for a while then got a ride with Jason back to Erika's once Nick, Terry and Jesse showed. They were all freaked out – not because there was an accident or because people were fighting – but because their boyfriends weren't doting on them. Ugh."

"It was so sweet how Landi stayed with me," Dillan said, smiling to herself.

"What was up with you last night? Before all of the Terry and Jesse drama?" Tyann asked.

Dillan shrugged, not too sure herself.

"It hurt to see him with her, huh?"

"Yeah, I can't help it. I guess it's just old baggage."

"Oh, please. You're still in love with him." Tyann stated.

"No, I'm not."

"Yes, you are," she insisted.

"No, I'm really not. It's just past stuff creeping up on me. Once I get used to the way things are now, I'll be fine. It's just something I have to work through Ty, I swear. I'm *not* in love with him."

"Whatever you say."

"Ty, you brat! I'm not!"

Tyann giggled. "You don't have to get so

defensive."

"I'm not defensive!"

"No, just confused," she said, lovingly patting Dillan on the head.

Goof ♡

Landi felt a hand caress his face as he slowly awoke, still exhausted from the night before. The first thing that popped into his sleepy thoughts was Dillan. He'd relived the horror of her crash in his mind too many times. It had scared the shit out of him. The thought of losing her...

He opened his eyes to see Beth with a sweet smile staring back at him. She looked fresh, awake and ready for a fashion show.

"Hi," she whispered.

"Hey." A little confused, he stretched and looked at her again in the light of day coming through his bedroom window. Was he dreaming?

"It's almost three in the afternoon, I figured you'd want to get up."

"When did you get here?" he asked, propping his head up on his arm.

"A few minutes ago. I missed you last night." She ran a hand along his bare chest.

"You mean, you're not mad at me?"

Her texts and phone calls following the accident seemed to have said otherwise.

"I can't be mad at you for being a caring compassionate person – even if your ex is involved."

Good thing she doesn't know about the dinner.

He raised a suspicious eyebrow at her, causing her to giggle.

"What?"

"Okay, who are you and what have you done with my girlfriend?"

She laughed. "Come on, I'm not *that* bad."

He gave her a cynical look.

"I'm not!" She insisted. "All right, so maybe I was a little irritated at first..."

"Irritated? You kinda ripped me a new one last night."

"Oh, don't be so dramatic." She playfully pushed him. "I talked to Erika about it and she made me realize that there was nothing to be upset about."

"Good..."

Beth stopped his words with a big sexy kiss. He was wide-awake.

"Drama queen," he teased, getting straddled.

"So, we're having dinner at my parents tonight."

Landi moaned. He'd rather have a root canal.

"It'll be fun."

"I don't know if I can handle that tonight, after last night."

"Don't worry, there'll be plenty of alcohol, as always." She kissed his nose. "And if you're a good boy I'll give you a little bonus before." She ground her hips into his making him forget about the world.

"And after?"

"You're pushing it," she said, removing her shirt to expose taut breasts. Within seconds they were in the midst of a midday sack session.

Once showered and completely awake, Landi found himself thinking of Dillan again. He was worried about her. He knew, even before the accident, that she had been upset but he wasn't sure why. He had watched her drink like a fish, not enjoy the fireworks very much, and then walk out of the bathroom with bloodshot eyes. He couldn't help but wonder.

After spending a little time with his mom, Landi survived another formal fancy dinner with Beth's parents in the richest neighborhood in Boise. He hated everything about it. Her dad was a successful lawyer who golfed on weekends and had bourbon with his men's club more often than not. Beth's mom wasn't much better. She was cold, stiff and stuck in the fifties. Their precious only daughter was their life – their key to more success. It was clear that they disapproved of Landi since he wasn't a clean-cut law student with a golf hobby and stick up his ass. Landi knew he didn't belong anywhere near this family. His phone trilled giving him a much needed break.

Dillan: Hey Goof. I'm good. Just letting you know I survived the night. ;-)

Landi: Glad to hear you're okay. TTYL.

The next day, on his way up the hill to Tyann and Jason's, Landi's mind was filled with thoughts of Dillan. He couldn't seem to shake wondering how she was doing. He'd even seriously thought about going to see her. He told himself he'd text her later.

Tyann answered the door wearing a neon yellow bathing suit with a beach towel wrapped around her waist. Landi smiled. She was just the person he wanted to see.

"Hi, Landi. Come on in."

He followed her to the living room where she yelled for Jason.

"He's changing, we just went for a swim."

"Cool. How is everything?"

"Good."

"How's Di?"

"She's doing better, resting. Have you guys been texting?"

"She sent me a text last night but I was busy so I couldn't really...respond."

"You should call her, she's bored."

Landi sat in their recliner and ignored the comment. So many thoughts and questions circled in his head, he tried to pick out the important ones. "What was she upset about at the party?"

Tyann sat on the armrest of the couch and sighed. "She's just trying to adjust to everything, you know? Get used to the way things are now."

What does that mean?

"What do you mean?"

"Hey man! What's up?" Jason walked out with a slaphappy grin. His blue eyes were glazed over and smiling. Landi knew that look all too well.

Swim, my ass.

"You ready to head out?" They had planned to go to Jesse's for a much needed guy's night.

"Yeah, give me two more seconds."

Tyann stood and walked to the kitchen. Landi followed, not even close to being done with the conversation.

"What do you mean, Ty? She's trying to get *used*

to things?"

She gave him an overly cynical look. "Like you don't know? You and Beth. She's never seen you with another female…ever."

It hit him – hard. He felt like a total dumbass. "Oh."

Tyann poured herself some iced tea and offered him some but he was too busy thinking of just the right way to ask his next question.

"You know Di's surfing accident?"

She turned to him with a frown. "What surfing accident?"

Exactly my point.

Tyann quickly covered. "Oh, yeah?"

He nodded.

"What?"

"You're just as bad a liar as she is. What really happened?"

Tyann suddenly looked uncomfortable. Her face flushed as she gulped down her iced tea – a rare trait for Tyann. "You need to talk to her about it."

"Is she okay?"

"She's fine, but it would be best if you just left it alone."

"What's the big deal?"

"Why do you care so much, anyway? Do you still have feelings for her?"

"I just want to know what happened, that's all. And yes, I do care about her. Why is that such a bad thing?"

"It's not…" Tyann sighed.

Jason walked in looking curious. "You ready?"

Landi said goodbye to Tyann and got into Jason's car feeling worse than he had minutes earlier.

"What's going on?" Jason asked as they drove to Jesse's.

"You know anything about Di's surfing accident?"

Jason frowned. "No."

"Have you seen that big scar on her back?"

"No...maybe. I don't know."

Landi sighed, and then explained what he knew. "...I know something bad happened to her."

Jason was unusually quiet for a few minutes, and then he spoke up.

"I remember Tyann being really upset a few years ago when Di was still in Cali...actually it was right before she broke up with you. Tyann was devastated but she wouldn't tell me what was wrong. I knew it had something to do with Di because she would be on the phone with her then start balling. I was really worried about her and tried to get her to tell me anything, but she wouldn't. That must have been it, whatever it was."

"Well, what the fuck was it?"

"I don't know man, but would you really want to know? If it was something that bad? Maybe you should just leave it alone. She'll tell you if she feels she needs to."

"I guess, but..."

But what if *it* was the answer to the question he'd been asking himself for years – why did she break up with him in the first place? So hatefully and harshly after they'd been in love for years.

Landi was plagued by 'what ifs' all the way to Jesse's. He couldn't figure out why it bothered him so much and that bothered him even more.

As the guys talked and drank in Jesse's living room that evening, Landi drowned the feelings away with alcohol hoping they wouldn't surface again.

Shoo ♡

Dillan's bruises began to heal and fade but Terry's wounded heart was damaged. She was severely depressed, sick, barely eating and not speaking to anyone, so Dillan found herself watching Tibby before and after work on most days, feeling ridiculously overwhelmed.

She and Landi had been texting off and on since the accident, which made her happy, but she really wanted to see him more than anything. She kept meaning to call him but was up to her ears in work, stress and babysitting, taking naps in her spare time. Pathetic.

Luckily on a Friday afternoon, Tyann offered to watch Tibby while Dillan got some time to do whatever she wanted.

Freedom!

Her first thought was to stop by Landi's, but instead she found herself at the old house, sitting on the front step with her dad who was taking a break from lawn mowing. She inhaled the sweet smell of fresh cut grass and invigorated earth. Luckily, a breeze had cooled down the heat from the day so it was the perfect temperature for a summer afternoon.

Her father smiled wearing his old sweaty t-shirt and ball cap. He ruffled her hair with his work gloves causing grass shavings to fly.

"Why don't you get Nick to do this for you?" Dillan asked, shaking the grass from her hair. "Make him do the hard work."

"Oh, I like getting my hands dirty every once in a while." He grinned. "How's the new place?"

"Good, I've been wanting to paint but I haven't had the time. Plus, I'm not too sure on the colors yet."

"Well, whenever you're ready I'll be happy to help."

"Sounds good." She smiled at her beloved father taking in his features and presence. Moments like these meant the world to her. "How have things been around here?"

"Same old," he said. "Nothing too exciting ever happens around here anymore, speaking for myself and your mother, I mean. Your brother is a whole different story."

Dillan laughed out loud. "Kick his butt out of the house, he needs it."

"I'm working on it."

Dillan gazed up at the bronzing sky through the limbs of the big tree, ignoring the passing cars on the street ahead.

"Looks like your boy came to see his mother for the day."

She looked at her dad who was shamelessly pointing down the road at Landi getting out of his truck. He glanced their way to see them staring at him. Dillan wanted to die. Landi waved and her dad waved back, then he disappeared inside.

"Go get him!" he teased.

"Dad…"

"Ahh, come on, don't be shy. Go see if he needs help."

Dillan was shooed off the lawn toward Jan's wondering what she was going to say. Not to mention the fact that she hadn't dressed as if she would be seeing anyone other than her family. Why had she chosen the grungy t-shirt and shorts ensemble?

She'd just stepped onto the front porch when Landi walked out.

"She's resting," he said, as if already knowing she was there. Dillan was pleased to see him looking just as grungy in a t-shirt and baggy-ish pants.

They walked as if it were completely natural onto the lawn in the shade of a tree. "How are things going?" Landi asked, searching her face with gentle eyes.

"Life's been crazy lately."

"So I've heard. How's the head?"

"Back to normal, whatever that is." She got a grin out of him, which made her smile. "How are you?"

"Good," he plucked a leaf from the tree.

Dillan had a nagging urge that just wouldn't go away. "You want to go on a walk with me?"

"Now?" he asked.

"Yeah."

"Where?"

"Just around here…like old times."

He looked hesitant, but said, "All right."

As they walked down Collister, Landi was quiet and guarded. Dillan wasn't sure what to think, hoping her plan wasn't a mistake.

She led them one street over from Collister on a familiar route to the creek, a tiny little flow of water next to a dirt path behind some houses. Besides being the place where they first met, it was a place they would go to meet and hang out all the time as kids. They had even made love there once.

When they got to their sacred spot, Dillan took a deep breath, smelling the fragrant air. The scent of flowers, creek water and dry grass brought her back to her teen years.

"I haven't been here in...forever." Landi said, sitting in the dirt beside the creek. He tossed a few stones in.

Dillan sat beside him as they watched the water ripple. She couldn't help but think about their so many memories and she laughed out loud, getting a reaction out of Landi.

"What?" he asked, chuckling right along with her.

"I was just remembering how young and stupid we were."

They talked about good times they'd shared as Landi slowly opened up. The two laughed and giggled, reminiscing about the past until Landi got quiet again.

"Why do you do this to me?" he asked, with hurt in his eyes.

Dillan began to worry. "Do what?"

"You bring me here and make me remember and feel all these things, why?"

For a second she was speechless.

"Why is it such a bad thing?"

He didn't answer. Instead he stood looking mad.

"What's wrong?" She stared up at a scowling

Landi.

"What are you trying to do?"

"What do you mean? I'm not trying to do anything." She stood and faced him.

"Bullshit. You can't just come back and expect everything to be like it was when we were sixteen."

Dillan's heart sank. She couldn't help but get upset. "I don't, Landi. But I did expect you to still be a friend! Ever since I've been back you've been distant and weird."

"Distant and weird?" He snapped. "Pulling you out of a wreck, inviting you to dinner and giving you my phone number is considered distant and weird?"

Dillan realized he had a point.

"Consider yourself lucky," he added.

"Excuse me?" Dillan asked. Now she was pissed.

"You're lucky I even give you the time of day after what you did to me!"

That was it.

"Are you fucking kidding me right now?" Dillan shouted, feeling her face flame. "Guess what, asshole? Just because life hasn't gone your way doesn't mean you get to go around feeling sorry for yourself! I've been hurt too, it sucks, but I didn't shut everything out and I sure as hell didn't forget about you and me, because that is still one of the best things that has ever happened to me!" By now she was screaming and Landi looked even more pissed.

"Well, maybe you should get over it!"

Tears came to her eyes. "Screw you!"

Landi turned and walked away, abandoning her as she had abandoned him. Dillan cried uncontrollably, shedding layers of pain that hadn't yet been processed.

She was beyond devastated from his words and reactions. It was as if he didn't care about their past or history at all. As if it had been erased in his world. It tore her apart.

She fell in the dirt and cried for what felt like forever, then slowly walked home. Landi's truck was long gone by the time she got into her car and sped away.

Old Times ♡

She started the whole thing! She shouldn't have taken me there to begin with. It's all her fault!

A playback of the heated fight and what was said ran over and over in Landi's mind as he drove aimlessly around town. He stopped at a local park and walked along a path trying to rationalize but all that came to mind was Dillan's innocent, teary eyes looking up at his.

He knew he had been an asshole, a raging one. His suppressed emotions had backfired and got the best of him. He needed to apologize to her.

As he walked further he began to feel guilt and the need to see her again, to make everything all right. A picture of her crying in the dirt popped into his head as he quickly walked back to his truck.

How could I have left her like that?

Seven minutes later he was back on Collister Drive, but her car was gone. He dialed her number – no answer. She was ignoring him. Good idea.

Just for a second he contemplated driving to her

townhouse but went home instead. He had chores to do.

Where is she? Why do I care? I don't care.

Landi unloaded the dishwasher, started some laundry and took the trash out but his mind kept wandering back to Dillan. He was so distracted he broke a glass, forgot to put soap into the washing machine and threw the garbage bag into the recycling bin.

He was out the door and in front of Dillan's townhouse within minutes. Her Accord was parked outside, which already made him feel better.

He walked around the small stone path to her front door, which was vibrating with sound. He knocked once, then twice and after two more times, let himself in.

Music flooded throughout the space. A familiar smell caught Landi's attention. Fresh paint. He followed the smell and the sound…and nearly had a heart attack.

Dillan was practically naked painting away with a roller, her back to him. She was wearing nothing but a skimpy white tank top and lacy blue underwear. She looked like she was on a mission, taking some aggression out on the living room wall.

Landi couldn't help but grin.

He admired her ass, hips, waist, thighs… and every other part of her backside until she stopped to wipe hair from her face.

"Shit!" She jumped nearly a foot in the air when she saw him. With a scowl she walked to the stereo, turned it down, then set the roller in a tray next to three gallons of paint.

"What are you doing?" he asked, unable to control his roving eyes.

"What am *I* doing? What the hell are you doing?" she yelled. "You scared the shit out of me!"

"I'm sorry, your door was unlocked. You weren't answering." He reached out and wiped paint from her chin. That expression made him want to touch her again... all over. He wondered if she was thinking the same thing as they stared at each other for a moment. Then she looked down at herself.

"Hold on." Two seconds later she came back with shorts on and picked up the roller to smooth cool blue paint onto the wall.

"Di, you don't have to paint your whole house just because you're pissed at me."

She burst out laughing. "This has nothing to do with you."

"You want some help?"

She glanced at him without a word as he took off his shirt and picked up a paintbrush.

"I'm sorry," he said.

She kept on painting.

"I didn't mean what I said. It's just..."

"What?" she snapped as they both stopped what they were doing and stared at each other.

"You have to understand that I shoved all those memories and feelings aside because it was too painful for me to think about it all the time. It's really hard to go back to them. It was overwhelming being there again, does that make sense?"

"It makes perfect sense," she said. "I just thought..." She choked tears back and tried to distract herself with painting. "I was an idiot to think that you would be happy to see me. All I wanted was for us to be good friends again, like we used to be. Maybe you're right, I do need to get over it."

He walked to where she stood and grabbed her

painting arm. She stopped to face him. "I'm glad you came back, but...I'm still mad."

"I know." Dillan looked remorseful.

"It was just...crazy, Di. It was crazy. And I still don't understand."

Landi remembered how in love they were – ridiculously, recklessly and wholeheartedly in love. He had plans to marry her. Went to visit her every chance he got at her college in California, determined not to let the distance between them cause a rift. Everything was great...until she called him out of the blue and tore his heart and soul out. Then she ran away to Mexico leaving him devastated all over again.

"I was stupid, I know." Dillan admitted. "And I know I hurt you. I'm so sorry for that. I guess I just needed to experience the world for myself."

"Why won't you tell me the truth?"

Color drained from Dillan's cheeks. Her green eyes widened. "What do you mean?"

"I know something happened. Something that caused you to act the way you did."

"Yeah, I fell in love with someone else."

Landi shook his head. "Bullshit. You haven't had sex with anyone in three years."

Dillan went back to painting, hiding any expression she was displaying.

"I'm sorry. I don't want to make you uncomfortable or get in a fight. I just know that something isn't right and I wish you would talk to me."

Dillan turned to look at him. Sadness was evident... and something deeper.

Landi's stomach lurched. He hated seeing her upset. He wanted to wrap her in his arms and comfort her.

"I can't."

He was speechless. He hadn't expected that.

"So you admit that there's more to what happened than what you told me?"

"Yes."

Landi finally felt like he was getting somewhere. "Does it have something to do with your surfing accident?"

"I don't want to talk about it anymore," she said, shutting down. "I need you to respect that."

He nodded and picked up a brush. "I can do that."

Landi tried his best to change the subject to lighter topics. Within minutes he had her laughing.

"Di, I really am glad that you came back."

"Thank you." Her eyes brightened as she smiled at him. "That means a lot."

They talked for hours painting away, getting caught up on moments missed and things that needed to be said for so long.

By the time the sun began to rise, they were getting giddy and goofy, laughing like teens. It was like old times again, just a little different.

L.O.V.E. ♡

Dillan awoke at noon with a new fuzzy feeling and came to a painful realization. The first thing she did after getting dressed and scarfing down a bagel was drive to Tyann's to share it with her.

Landi's truck was parked in the driveway giving Dillan unexpected butterflies. She was glad to have a cute flouncy tank top and tight jeans on.

She let herself in finding Tyann, Jason and Landi lounging out back on the deck in the warm mid-morning sun. Tibby ran around in the grass and was the first to notice her. The little redhead grabbed her leg giving it a tight squeeze. Dillan wondered why Jason and Tyann were watching her.

"Hi sweetie." Dillan picked her up and poked her tummy before Tibby wriggled out of her hold, off and running again.

"Hey, girlie." Tyann grinned at her behind chic shades and a sun hat. Something told her she already knew her secret.

Dillan sat in an empty chair beside Landi who gave her the sweetest smile. All she could think about was how hot he had looked the night before painting shirtless with his pants barely hanging on – his adorable buns teasing her.

"What are you up to today?" Jason asked.

"Nothing at all."

"Did you get any sleep after I left?" Landi asked with a devilish grin. If he was trying to give their friends the impression that they'd had sex he'd succeeded.

"Not much."

Tibby brought her and Tyann flowers from the garden then sat in Landi's lap. He hugged and poked her playfully. The gesture surprised Dillan. She'd never seen him so paternal. It made her love him even more.

"Where's Terry?" Dillan asked.

Tyann widened her eyes. Bad topic. "She's not feeling well."

"So, guess who's in town for a while?" Jason asked, tactfully changing the subject.

"Who?"

"Charlie."

"Seriously?"

"Yeah, he called and wants to get together with everybody."

"How long will he be here?" Dillan asked.

"I don't know, it sounds like it might be for a while."

Dillan smiled to herself thinking of their old friend. Charlie had always been the ball of energy in their clan and a total player in high school. He ended up going to California for college and never returned, except for the occasional visit. Dillan hadn't seen him since the

Christmas before last when she learned he had become a successful engineer, wasn't married and was still a big partier. She was excited to see him again.

The four friends talked about Charlie and memories from the past until Landi stood and stretched giving Dillan a peek of his happy trail. She had the urge to poke his stomach.

"Alright, I've got to go check on my mom," he said.

"Can I join you?" Jason asked.

"Of course."

Tyann stood to give Jason a big hug and kiss as Dillan and Landi remained in an awkward silence. It seemed strange to not kiss him goodbye next to their lovebird friends.

"I'll see you later," Landi said. "Text me."

"I will. Tell your mom I said hi."

As soon as the men disappeared through the back gate Tyann gave Dillan a huge, maniacal grin.

"What?"

"How'd the painting go?"

Dillan couldn't control the grin that spread over her face. "He told you?"

"Yeah, that he got in trouble with his girlfriend for coming home at six in the morning covered in paint."

"Oh." She laughed, finding the image amusing.

"So what happened between you two? What's the big secret?"

"Well..." Dillan told her all about the walk, the fight, the insane amount of painting and most of what was said.

"Wow, he opened up to you." Tyann stated.

"Yeah, and I did too."

"What do you mean?"

Dillan told her about his realization and her confession that there was something bigger and deeper underneath the surface.

"You told him the truth?" Her eyes were huge.

"No, but he knows there's more."

Tyann sat back in her seat. "Yeah, he asked me about the accident the other day."

"I don't know if I can keep it from him much longer," Dillan confessed. "But I also don't think I can tell him, Ty. It would kill *me* - imagine what it would do to him? I don't want to lose him. I'm just getting him back."

"Oh, honey. It's all right." Tyann removed her hat and combed her fingers through her long silky hair. "You don't have to say anything. It's your decision. Either way it'll be okay."

"Yeah, well... there's another problem."

"What's that?"

"I'm in love with him."

Tyann's eyes widened again except this time she jiggled with excitement. "Di!"

"I didn't realize it until last night but I just can't help it, I love him, in a new and different way. It's all still there. I've been trying to deny it for so long but every time I see him my feelings grow stronger." Dillan leaned back in her chair and looked up at the cloudless sky. "I'm completely insane, aren't I?"

"No." Tyann chuckled. "You never got over him Di, and he never got over you."

"Do you think he ever thinks about me?"

"Are you fricking kidding me? Of course he thinks about you! Why do you think he was so bent out of shape about you coming back? He's fighting himself, his true feelings."

"I just don't know what to do." Dillan eyed her beautiful friend.

"Spend more time with him, flirt a little, see how he reacts."

"But I don't know if it's right or if I should. I'm happy just having him back in my life. I don't want to screw up this new friendship. If he doesn't feel the same that's okay with me, really."

"Then just be a friend, take things slow and see where it goes from there. You'll know if he's feeling you."

Dillan was lost in thought when Tibby ran up to her with handfuls of grass. She threw it in the air giggling at herself.

"Di, we have to help Terry, she's in really bad shape." Tyann said.

"I know. Where the hell is Jesse?"

"Trying to figure out how to get his head out of his ass."

Dillan laughed.

"Whatever you do, don't tell her Charlie's in town. No need to stir things up between those two just yet."

"Got it."

Terry had been just another girl who fell into the Charlie trap in high school. She had lost her virginity to him only to find out he was cheating on her, but it was soon forgotten once Terry found Jesse. As adults, Terry and Charlie quickly got over the high school drama becoming chummy friends, always standing a little too long or staring a little too hard.

"Let's take her out." Tyann suggested, twisting her mane into a ponytail. "Jesse has Tibbs tonight so we can steal Terry."

"Okay, but first I need a nap."

That evening, Terry's two closest friends went on a mission, determined to get her out of the house and into an upbeat setting.

Dressed to kill in heels and thick makeup Tyann and Dillan drove to Terry's apartment and pounded on the door. Terry eventually let them in looking like a wreck. Her red hair was frazzled, there were bags under her eyes and it seemed she'd been wearing the same pajamas for days as she cried to them.

"We're getting you the hell out of this apartment," Tyann said, nearly tripping over one of Tibby's toys in an attempt to open a window in her five-inch heels. Dillan laughed under her breath. "We're going to go out and have fun and you are going to move on!"

"I can't," Terry cried, flopping onto her couch. "I don't want to."

"Too bad, you're coming out with us, whether you like it or not!" She shot Dillan a grin.

"I'm going to be a single mom for the rest of my life," Terry wailed. "And nobody's ever going to love me!"

"Not if you look like that."

Forty-five minutes later, Tyann and Dillan had Terry looking like a supermodel in a tight, sapphire blue mini-dress with her red hair down and wispy around her shoulders. Her eyes were dark and smoky. Her lips, tinted with light lip gloss, screamed kiss me. Every guy at the classy local bar was drooling over her. Dillan quickly ordered Terry a chocolate raspberry martini, while she got herself a fuzzy navel and Tyann a classic cosmo. Not five minutes later, Terry had a hot guy hitting on her.

Landi: Hey booger face.
Dillan: What's up turd licker?
Landi: You make me smile :)

Dillan laughed at her and Landi's text exchange. They were so mature.

Tyann and Dillan sipped on their drinks watching Terry laugh and toss her hair at the bar as if she were some entertaining actress in a movie. Guys flocked like pigeons buying her drink after drink.

After only an hour it was evident that Terry was at her limit. Her voice had gone up an octave.

"You know we're going to have to cut her off soon," Tyann said, her eyes glued to The Terry Show.

"Yep."

Dillan had just about finished her peach schnapps and orange juice when a hand pet her ponytail.

"Is that a keg in your pants, cause I'd *love* to tap that ass."

Dillan turned ready to kill.

Charlie grinned back at her.

"You shithead! Oh my God! What are you doing?" She stood to hug him getting pulled into a big bear embrace. They'd always had a strong connection. She could honestly say that besides Landi, Charlie was her best guy friend.

"You should have seen your face!" He laughed, getting a kick out of himself. "What's up, Ty?" He hugged her then joined them at the table, sitting backward in a chair Charlie style.

"Did you just get into town or what?" Tyann asked.

"Yeah, I got here this morning. Thought I'd check out the night life, you know me."

"And you didn't call us? What the hell, dick."

He laughed, cute as ever. In addition to having an amazing personality he was also physically attractive in a guys-guy sort of way. Charlie was a hunk with a lean, muscular build women would kill for. His arms were about as big as Dillan's upper thighs and he had no problem showing off his assets wearing A-shirts ninety percent of the time. Beneath a backward baseball cap were deep blue eyes and short dirty blond hair. He was a vision.

"So, where are the guys?" he asked.

"It's just us," Tyann said. "Girls night out."

"Aww, I crashed your party."

"No, you didn't," Dillan said. "You blend right in."

Charlie tickled her ribs. "Thanks, D."

Dillan couldn't resist stealing his cap.

Dillan: OMG   Charlie's   here!   We're hanging out with him.

Landi: No shit?

Dillan: Crazy, huh?

As they talked and caught up, Dillan noticed Terry looking drunker by the minute. Tyann and Dillan silently communicated this fact then Tyann went to control the situation. Charlie and Dillan had some time alone.

"So what are you up to these days?" Dillan asked, giving her long lost friend a smile.

"I've got an awesome job working with a big company out in Cali, which I'm totally digging." He paused to take a swig of beer. "Right now I'm trying to decide if I want to buy a house. I'd kind of like to have one here eventually, so I can travel back and forth, you know?"

Dillan nodded, taking a sip of a new drink. "How long are you out here?"

"I took most of the summer off to visit for a while and maybe check out the real estate."

"Ah, so the money's good?"

"Oh yeah, really good." He smiled, looking into her eyes. "So what about you?"

She told him all about her current situation: moving back, her job and the townhouse.

"What's it like coming back? Is it weird?" he asked.

"No, I'm glad to be here."

"That's good." He gave her a mischievous look. "So, I hear there's been some tension between you and Landi? How's that going?"

"Fine, we're just friends. It's been interesting getting adjusted to the new grown-up us, but it's okay."

"Yeah, I finally proposed to April, but she got scared."

"She turned you down?"

He nodded. "She can't get over our past. I just wanted to fix what I fucked up but it's all over now. She can't trust me."

April had been his high school sweetheart who he ended up cheating on, which had completely devastated her. She moved away and he never got over it, chasing her for years.

Dillan could see the pain in his eyes as he drank his beer. She thought about Landi and herself when they were young and remembered some of their not-so-happy moments. Those memories made her remember how much they loved each other and how committed they were.

She sighed, missing it… missing him when Terry's voice suddenly filled her ears.

"Holy shit! Charlie?"

His eyes just about bugged out of his head as he stood to embrace her.

"What's up, girl?"

"What the hell are you doing here?" Terry

laughed. "I didn't know you were in town."

"Yeah, I..." Charlie's voice trailed off as they walked to the bar together, laughing and chattering.

Tyann and Dillan shrugged, then sat at their table and ordered food and another round of drinks.

By three in the morning, Tyann and Dillan were sober enough to drive Terry and Charlie, who were making out like horny teenagers in the back seat, to Terry's apartment. They watched them disappear inside, knowing without a doubt what was going to happen. Laughter ensued.

Their friend got exactly what she needed, just not from whom they'd expected it.

Nitty Gritty ♡

Do you have any idea where my wife is? Jesse's text was unusually serious.

Landi: I have no idea.

Jesse: She's not answering her phone, I've been trying to call all morning.

Landi: Sorry man. I don't know. You might want to ask one of the girls.

All Landi could think about as he lay in bed alone was everything he and Dillan had said to one another within the last couple days. He didn't know whether to be mad or grateful that she had opened up his mind and heart to a lot of things he'd been ignoring. Pieces of himself that he forgot existed were coming back to life.

He decided to drive up the hill in the hot morning sunshine to talk to the only person who would understand.

Jason was out front mowing the lawn in shorts and a t-shirt, his dark hair disheveled. The sight made Landi chuckle. Jason and yard work didn't mix. Even as a teen he'd never been good at any kind of manual labor.

"Hey! You want to do mine, too?" Landi teased, walking in front of the mower.

Jason shut it down and smiled at his best friend, wiping away the sweat from his brow.

"What are you doing?" Landi asked. "Don't you have servants for this?"

"Ha, ha, smart ass. No, I enjoy mowing the lawn on occasion. What are you up to?"

"Not much. Holy shit though I got the weirdest text from Jesse about Terry..." Jason chuckled, removing his sunglasses.

"What?"

"Terry, Charlie..."

"Aw crap, I didn't even think about it."

"Yeah, according to Tyann they've been humping like bunnies since last night when they apparently ran into each other at a bar."

Landi laughed, remembering Dillan's text. "Have you eaten, man? I'm starving."

"Help me finish and we'll go out?"

"Deal."

Doing yard work with Jason reminded Landi of his childhood. The two were like blood brothers, having known each other since birth. Each of them had lost their father's at a young age. They'd survived together through drug addiction, abuse and tragedy. Their bond was for life – supportive, loyal and unconditional.

The two did what they'd done a thousand times before – teamed up to get the job done. Once the lawn was pristine and the tools had been put away, they sat on the front porch steps drinking ice water.

"Where's Tyann?" Landi asked.

"At the studio with Dillan."

"She's dancing now?" That vision made him warm.

"I think she's just checking out a few classes, keeping Tyann company."

"Oh."

Jason raised an eyebrow with half a smirk. "What's been up with you? Did something happen between you and Di?"

For once he was glad that Jason was asking questions. "We had a heated discussion and resolved some things."

"That's good."

"Yeah, but I'm still really confused about something."

Jason looked intrigued. He sipped his water as Landi explained her strange confession.

"Okay, so let me ask you something," Jason said. "If this *thing* forced her to break it off with you for whatever reason, what would you think?"

"I'd hate myself...for not trying harder or..." Landi's throat tightened. "I've blamed her all these years."

"Do you still have feelings for her?"

"Maybe."

Jason grinned. He knew the real answer. "And you're not sure how you feel about it?"

Landi wasn't surprised that his best friend was right on. He sighed, running a hand through his hair before replying.

"I just don't know what to do. There's nothing I can do if she won't talk to me. I have to rely on what I know — that she broke it off with me and there's some strange mystery behind it."

Jason nodded. "So now what?"

"Nothing. We remain acquaintances...friends, whatever."

"Hmm."

"What?"

"Would you consider giving her a chance? I mean, if she still has feelings for you and wants to try it out again?"

"No...I don't know."

Jason wasn't about to let him get away with that answer. "Come on, man."

"I'd have to know the truth – all of it. Every nitty gritty detail before I could even consider it."

"That's fair."

Landi was glad when Jason stood and suggested they go eat. The talk hadn't gone exactly the way Landi had hoped. He was more confused than ever.

♡

"You're still in love with her, aren't you?" Beth screamed, tossing clothes all over Landi's bedroom floor. She looked like a rabid beast. Landi wasn't sure he'd ever seen her so pissed.

"I am not. Would you stop?"

"I hate how you guys are friends. You're all buddy-buddy now. I can only take so much of this shit!"

Landi sighed, angry at himself for not erasing the texts from Dillan. Beth had read every one of them.

"I can't believe you gave her your phone number, Landi. Seriously? You're texting your ex now?" She pinned him with an accusatory look.

"She's a friend, Beth. That's all. Would you please

calm down?"

"Everything was so much better when you hated her."

"For who?"

"Everyone!"

Anger began to rise. "No, you know what the problem is? You don't trust me, and I'm fucking sick of it! You're always all God damned paranoid I'm doing shit behind your back, with her!"

"Do I not have good reason?" she yelled. "You're perfect little high school sweetheart moves back and suddenly you're best friends again!"

It took all Landi had to not kick her out then and there. There was a long silence as they both calmed a little.

Beth cracked, falling onto the bed. "It's not that I don't trust you, it's just really hard for me, this whole thing."

Landi felt terrible seeing tears stream down her face. He wrapped her in his arms and kissed her face. "I know, baby. I'm sorry."

"It's okay, I just…I need you." She devoured him with kisses and her magical sexual ways, distracting Landi from everything but how good she made him feel. He only felt slightly guilty when Dillan popped back into his mind the minute he and Beth parted.

♡

Dillan: If you get a minute this week, I need help with my new TV.

Landi had played it cool all week, being a loyal boyfriend to Beth who was in dire need of his love and attention. He'd ignored Dillan's texts until she asked for help. He couldn't resist.

He waited until Thursday evening after work since Beth would be with friends and unaware of his detour. A thunderstorm rolled in electrifying the air as he was driving to Dillan's. It only made Landi more invigorated. Maybe the storm would be so bad he'd be stranded with Dillan for days. The thought made him smile.

Dillan answered the door looking sleepy and wearing a pair of small shorts and tank top. He took all of her in with one glance. Her golden ponytail, makeup-less face, amazing body...

"It's raining," he said.

"I noticed."

She seemed a bit hesitant as he stepped in and looked around. He wondered why.

"Your place is looking good. I like the paint job."

A smile was exactly what he wanted and exactly what he got.

"Smartass."

Near the living room wall sat a huge quality entertainment center with a large flat screen TV cockeyed inside. Wires sprouted everywhere.

"That's why I asked for your help," she said, pointing to the contraption. "Nick got the TV working but it looks like shit. I know you're good at wiring so..."

"Yeah, I can do it." He took his flannel off and got right to work.

A half hour later the brand new entertainment center was in place, along with the TV, DVD player, receiver and surround system – all without any wires showing.

Dillan looked pleased as they sat on the couch, admiring how good it looked. Thunder boomed above.

"Thank you so much," she said with a smirk. "That

was driving me nuts."

"I bet it was. Miss Organization."

She playfully kicked him. "Mister Messy."

"Not anymore."

They stared each other down then cracked with laughter.

"You want to watch something?" she asked.

"Sure."

Halfway through the movie, Dillan sprawled out on the couch, resting her feet on Landi's legs like she used to when they were young. The gesture caused old memories to surface, along with an urge to tickle the hell out of her.

Landi stared down at her body, contemplating where to start first when a jolt of unexpected awareness hit him – hard. Her naked thighs, sexy stomach, large breasts... the incredible sex they used to have...

"Landi!"

Her foot slamming into his leg snapped him into the present. Di giggled at him, cheeks slightly flushed.

"Did you hear me?"

"No, what?"

"I said, don't even think about it."

He grinned. "I already did."

"I'll kick your ass."

The two glared each other down before playfully attacking, wrestling and pouncing throughout the house – all the while crying with laughter. As they giggled on the living room floor attempting to catch their breath a huge clap of thunder shook the house. Everything went black. Silence, then laughter.

"Oh my God," Dillan chuckled. "Now what?"

"Candles?"

They stumbled around the house in the glow of cell phone lights running into each other more than a few times looking for candles and matches. In total Dillan had three candles and one match left in a small book.

Landi carefully lit the candles and placed them on the coffee table before the couch. Dillan disappeared and came back with a blanket wrapped around herself.

"You cold?" he asked, finding her breathtakingly beautiful in the glow of candlelight.

"Yes, are you?"

He shrugged, getting wrapped inside the blanket with her. They sat before the table in silence sharing body heat and breathing rhythms, watching the candles flicker. It was incredibly peaceful.

"So much for entertainment," Dillan said with a grin.

Landi admired her profile, searching her face and expression in the shadowed lighting. It had been a long time since he'd been so intimate with her. He missed it. She turned to look at him, catching him off guard. Their faces so close caused a magnetic pull – an attraction natural and familiar. He wanted to kiss her, devour her with love. Everything in him screamed to go for it. Landi looked into her emerald eyes, searched her pouty lips, felt her breath on his. She smiled and nuzzled against his nose giving him all the permission he needed.

He gently caressed her face and pressed his lips against hers – sweet, innocent and soft. A flood of warmth enveloped his body. He was instantaneously fully aroused and ready for more…

Then his phone rang. The moment was broken.

Dillan looked away and distanced herself focusing hard on the candles. She was embarrassed.

"I can't," he said, not once taking his eyes off of her.

"I know. I'm sorry."

"Don't be. All you did was be cute." He pulled his phone from his pocket and saw "Missed call from Beth" on the screen. Of course.

"I wonder how long the power's going to be out?" Dillan said, keeping her gaze glued to the candles.

"Want to go for a walk in the rain?" Landi asked, needing to cool off. Plus, he knew the act would make Dillan happy. It was something they did all the time as kids.

She smiled at him and said, "Yes."

Any awkwardness was broken the minute they stepped out the door and ran down the block, giggling and playing in the giant raindrops. They were soaked in seconds having a blast just being together.

As they jumped through streams and stomped in puddles Landi realized exactly what had been missing in his life.

Happiness.

Dillan brought it out better than anyone.

Nightmare ♡

Dillan tossed and turned, plagued by visions she'd tried to forget. She wanted to escape but the terror dragged her further into the madness. Her never-ending nightmare….

Blurs of shadows and light melded together into one.

A haze she couldn't shake.

But he was there – holding her hand…tightly. Taking her somewhere…but where?

All she could see was blackness – an endless abyss.

Her body felt detached – limbs weak, flailing, numb. She couldn't feel much of anything. Was she walking? Floating?

No….

Pain ripped through her body like lightning. Every cell ached, screamed. She clawed for anything, anyone to save her.

But the hell continued, and her cries were unheard.

Lost.

Ignored.

If she survived, she'd never forgive herself.

If...

Palpable ♡

"**Y**eah! Girlfriend-free night!" Nick yelled, slapping hands with Landi who sat grinning in the backseat of Dillan's Accord. He was enjoying his view of the sexy blonde in the driver's seat. The afternoon sun beaming in through the windshield made her look that much more radiant.

"Is it that exciting?" Dillan asked, lowering her sunglasses to give her brother an apprehensive glance.

"Have you met Erika and Beth?"

"Nick! Don't be a dick. She's your girlfriend."

"He's got a point," Landi added. "They do get extra awkward when they're together."

"Yeah, like cliquey and snobby?" Dillan remarked. "I don't get what you guys see in them, honestly."

Nick and Landi exchanged an uber knowing guy grin that was ridiculously cliché.

"Wow," was all Dillan could add. "Where are they, anyway?"

"A bachelorette party."

"And you're not worried?"

"No," Nick laughed. "As long as she comes back to this..." He pointed to his body clothed in everything trendy. "I'm good."

Dillan smacked him, causing Landi to chuckle.

Jason was already firing up the grill for the Hawaiian themed BBQ when they arrived. Tyann made sure everyone was wearing a lei, which of course spawned the most ridiculous jokes. The backyard was embellished with bright, colorful decorations; the lawn freshly mowed and patio chairs strewn about. Music drifted throughout the yard and the refreshing pool sparkled in the sun's rays.

Landi grabbed a beer and happily mingled with Charlie, Jason and Nick in the backyard as the girls swarmed inside the house. He was glad when Dillan joined him with a beer and a smile.

"What are you doing?" she asked, bumping into his shoulder.

He laughed. "What are *you* doing?"

"Bothering you."

"You can't bother me."

"Wanna bet?"

"No."

They laughed at one another, locking eyes for more than a few seconds.

"What's up, D? You want to go for a swim?" Charlie grabbed her before she could answer and jumped in the pool. Landi watched as the two of them wrestled and played in the water feeling a rise of jealousy. He was envious of the relationship Charlie had with Dillan. He could touch and tease her at will – something Landi would kill to do.

Landi busied himself at the grill with Jason, all the

while keeping an eye on Dillan being chased by Charlie. She eventually made her way back to his side wearing dry clothes and holding a new drink. Any jealousy he'd felt melted as she kept him company throughout the evening. Everyone was having a great time eating, laughing and drinking up a storm around the patio and pool except Jesse, who arrived late and in a bad mood. It didn't help that Terry and Charlie were flirting like crazy, making things more than a little uncomfortable.

By the time dessert was over, it was safe to say that everyone was feeling a good buzz. The group migrated downstairs to the basement living room where there was a pool table, dart board, bar and sound system. Jason blasted music and poured drinks while Terry, Tyann, Nick and Charlie played a round of pool. Jesse sat at the bar with a scowl on his face while Dillan and Landi poked each other with pool sticks.

After slapping Landi's butt with her stick, Dillan walked up to him with a cute smile. "Wanna go get a drink with me?"

He couldn't control the grin that spread over his face.

She grabbed his hand and led him up the stairs away from the music, stumbling a bit on the last few steps.

"Whoa, are you okay?" he asked, wrapping his arm around her waist to steady her. Once again they were close – too close – staring at each other in the dim stairwell. His body responded. He had to quit putting himself in these situations.

She giggled, leaning into him even more. "I'm fine."

"I don't know if I believe you."

They burst into laughter.

"Don't pretend like you're not wasted. You've had more than me," she said.

He laughed. "Ok, you busted me. But at least I can walk straight."

"Dick." She teased, pushing herself away from him and up the last step.

They munched on peanuts and candy sharing swigs from a beer bottle as they ate.

Landi was downing the last of the beer when Dillan opened the freezer and dropped a piece of ice in his pants.

"Now try walking straight," she said.

Landi wriggled around to get it out while Dillan laughed hysterically.

"You think that's funny?" He pushed the icemaker and tossed slivers down her cleavage. Her gasp was priceless, then he realized he was in trouble.

"Oh shit."

Dillan grabbed the nearest drink on the counter and readied to toss it at him.

"Wait!" He yelled between cracks of laughter. "We're even. Let's call a truce."

"Okay..." She lowered the cup while he caught his breath. "After this!"

Coldness hit his man parts causing him to gasp for air. Landi caught Dillan in the unlit hallway near the guest bedroom. He tickled the crap out of her.

"Stop it!" she begged, barely able to talk. "Stop!"

"Not until you apologize!" he said, tickling her against the wall.

"Okay, I'm sorry."

"What? I can't hear you."

"I'm sorry!"

He finally stopped, allowing her to catch her breath as he examined his pants.

"Look! Look at this." He laughed, pointing to his crotch. "I look like I pissed myself."

They both cracked up.

"Now I have to go the rest of the night known as the man who pissed himself."

After another round of giggles Dillan looked up at him with big, passionate eyes. The shadows accentuated the contours of her face stirring an overwhelming desire in him.

"What?" he asked.

"You still know my secret spots."

"Of course I do. I miss playing with you. I could never do this with anyone else, not like I could with you."

They locked in a heavy gaze, mesmerized by the sexual tension dancing between them. There was no way to hide it. He craved her more than ever. Needed her love.

He reached out to tuck a golden lock behind her ear closing the gap between them, then she fell into his arms. She rested her head on his chest as they embraced, bodies entwined, fitting together in the perfect way that they had always had. Just feeling her body on his warmed his heart with a sensation he'd forgotten about. This was where he was meant to be. They stood in a loving hug, soaking in as much of each other as possible until Dillan looked up at him. He leaned in to kiss her but she stopped him with her finger.

"You can't, remember?"

He was about to protest when she grabbed his arm and led them back downstairs to the wild party.

"Where the hell have you two been?" Jason yelled, giving Landi a mischievous look. He handed him a beer and pool stick then Landi found himself thrown into a game of pool with Jesse and Jason.

"What happened? Where did you go?" Jason asked.

"Nothing. It was nothing."

"Bullshit."

"I'll tell you later."

Landi leaned over to shoot, getting a captivating smile from Dillan who was laughing with Nick and Tyann when something else caught his eye.

He looked up to see Terry and Charlie near the dartboard kissing like it was going out of style. Not just kissing. Terry had her arms wrapped around Charlie's neck as he held her small waist close to his body. It was sexual. Not a second later, Jesse was irate... and stomping toward them. Landi's stomach flipped.

"HEY!" Jesse yelled, immediately getting in Charlie's face. He pushed him but it barely had an effect on Charlie's muscular stature. "What the fuck is your problem?"

"I don't have a problem," Charlie answered, looking amused... and cocky.

"Jesse, stop it!" Terry yelled.

"Don't touch my wife!"

Terry got in his face. "Oh, don't even act like you care!"

"What? Is there a problem with that?" Charlie asked, finally showing some irritation.

"Yeah there's a problem, asshole! Don't fucking disrespect me like that!"

"Whoa! Knock it off you guys!" Jason yelled, getting between them. Landi dropped his stick and prepared to interfere.

140

"Disrespect, huh?" Charlie said. "How does it feel being on the other end, Jess? Does it hurt to know that your wife is being fucked by someone other than you?"

The room seemed to shift at the provocation.

Jesse pounced on Charlie and began hitting him relentlessly. Everything was a blur as Landi and Jason tried their hardest to pry them apart. No luck. Furniture snapped, glass shattered and blood flew.

It was a chaos tornado with no sign of an end.

"STOP!!!"

Everyone was yelling, doing their best to pry the two muscle heads off of each other when ice cubes and water exploded everywhere.

Landi looked up to see Tyann holding an empty cooler.

Finally, the fight was over.

Twenty minutes later, Charlie, Landi and Dillan were at her townhouse lounging in her living room trying to comprehend what had happened. Dillan knelt before Charlie on the couch, wiping his cuts as he held a bag of peas to his head.

"Well, at least I got laid," Charlie said with a smirk, holding up his floral necklace. He and Landi busted up laughing.

"I'm glad you put that asshole in his place," Dillan remarked. "He needed a taste of his own medicine."

"Glad to be of service."

Landi watched Dillan nurse Charlie feeling a twinge of jealousy again.

"You're so sweet, you know that?" Charlie said. "Why the hell this knucklehead didn't marry you is beyond me."

Dillan blushed.

"Do it, before it's too late."

"Shush, you need to rest."

Landi watched Dillan get up to wring out the washcloth in the kitchen as Charlie glanced at him. Charlie looked like a swollen version of himself.

"Seriously, dude," he said in a low voice. "Fuck the past, fuck everything – all that matters is what's in front of you right now."

Charlie's words hit Landi with a truth that was painfully accurate.

He's right.

Dillan came back wearing a t-shirt and shorts, her hair thrown up in a messy bun, make-up completely washed off. Landi's heart fluttered. She handed the washcloth to Charlie then sighed.

"I'm going to crash, guys. Feel free to watch TV, eat or do whatever you want. Keep those peas on your head."

"All right, babe. Thank you," Charlie said. "Love you, girl."

"Goodnight."

The second she disappeared Charlie widened his puffy eyes and pointed in Dillan's direction.

"Go!" he mouthed. "Go!"

Fearing Charlie might beat him up if he didn't comply, Landi stood and threw a pillow at him before slowly walking down the hallway toward Dillan's bedroom. Nerves wracked his stomach. What was he supposed to say? I want to be close to you. He did, very badly.

Dillan was lying in a poof of white blankets on her queen sized bed staring at her cell phone. A soft orange glow from the bedside lamp warmed the room.

"Goodnight," he said leaning ever so suavely on

the doorjamb.

Dillan busted up laughing. "Really?"

"Is it that bad?"

"Get your ass over here."

Landi jumped on the bed beside her. They stared at each other from across pillows – so close, yet so far away. He couldn't help but get lost in her amazing eyes. The intensity between them was palpable.

"What are you doing, troublemaker?" she asked with a smile.

"I want to be close to you."

"Just keep your lips to yourself." The silly look on her face made his heart swell.

"You're so beautiful," Landi heard himself say. "This is how I like you, just like this. You have no makeup on and your hair is tousled, but you're the most beautiful thing in the world to me."

Her cheeks flamed. "Landi…"

"I miss you, Di."

"You're drunk."

"I really do."

She looked deep into his eyes. "I miss you, too."

With that she closed the gap between them, nestling her head into his neck.

Landi's body exploded with sensations all over again. Something about Dillan's touch awakened him, made him alive and exhilarated. Complete.

He wrapped his arms around her and snuggled his face in her hair. Everything felt right in that moment.

Landi slowly closed his eyes, feeling as if he were in a dream.

Status ♡

Dillan awoke to a faint vibrating sound. She slowly opened her eyes to the morning sun, which made her head hurt...badly. Her stomach wasn't any better.

She sat up, realizing Landi was sound asleep beside her. His presence in her bed made her giddy. He looked so peaceful and comfortable, as if he'd slept there a thousand times. She smiled to herself having an urge to nestle into him but the vibrating sound wouldn't stop. It was coming from his pocket.

"Landi," she said, lightly pushing him. "You're vibrating."

He grunted and stretched then sat up, looking adorably exhausted and reached into his pocket, pulling out a cell phone. He studied it with sleepy eyes before falling back onto the bed.

"Fuck..." he moaned, putting a hand to his head.

"Feel like shit?"

"That's the least of my problems." He stood and adjusted his clothes. "Can you give me a ride up the hill?

Fast?"

Dillan wasn't sure what to say other than, "Sure."

Charlie slept away on Dillan's couch as she and Landi drove to Tyann and Jason's in the bright sun to retrieve his truck. The ride was quiet and a little awkward as Dillan wondered what was going on.

"What's wrong?" she asked, tipping up her sunglasses.

"Nothing."

She glanced at him for more but he sighed, staring straight ahead. He was annoyed. "I was supposed to be at a stupid brunch with Beth and her parents at ten thirty."

Dillan looked at the digital clock on her dash seeing it was ten after eleven.

"If it makes you feel any better, I missed Pilates."

He gave her a ridiculously cynical stare. "You're kidding right?"

Instead of answering the question she thought she'd try and lighten things. "Brunch, huh? You and that word don't mix."

But Landi apparently wasn't in the mood for jokes.

"You'll be fine, just tell them the truth..."

"The truth? Oh yeah, that's a really good idea. I got drunk and crashed in my ex-girlfriends bed, with her! But you know, it's no big deal."

"That's not what I meant."

"Whatever, I'm fucked either way."

Dillan was half relieved to see Landi's truck. She pulled up to the curb as Landi practically jumped out.

"Thanks," he yelled, just before slamming the door and running to his pickup. Dillan drove home hurt and a little angry. She didn't understand how Landi could be so distant after they'd connected so deeply. Just when she felt they were back to being their old selves their bond seemed lost all over again. She tried to tell herself that she had a combination of stress and a hangover but she still worried.

The last thing Dillan expected to see when she walked into her townhome was a buck naked Charlie. He stood in the middle of her living room toweling himself off.

"Hey, babe. Hope you don't mind I took a shower."

"I can see that." Dillan walked directly to the kitchen to make coffee eyeing his tight buns and rock hard abs. Charlie went about his business right in front of her, not seeming to care one way or another.

"Hey Charlie, there's this thing called drying yourself off in the bathroom. Ever heard of it?"

He grinned. "Is that coffee?"

"Yes, and you can have some as soon as you put some pants on," she said, focusing really hard on pouring water into the machine.

"I'm working on it," he said reaching for his carpenter jeans. "Did you take Landi home?

Dillan looked up and nodded, noticing Charlie's eye was pretty bruised.

"What happened between you two last night?" Charlie asked.

"What do you mean?

"I woke up to take a piss and you were snuggling, all wrapped up in each other like old times." He smirked, finally getting his shirt and pants all the way on.

"Yeah, well, he was pretty pissed off this morning."

"Ah, he's just stressed over his bitch of a girlfriend."

Dillan pondered it as she stirred milk and sugar into two mugs of coffee. She joined Charlie on the couch, handing him his steaming mug.

"I just don't understand how he can be so hot and cold." Dillan told Charlie all about their "kiss", intimate moment in the hallway, cozy snuggle before bed and how he'd turned into a stranger on the ride to his truck. Charlie seemed amused.

"I'm telling you, he loves the shit out of you, Di. His actions express it. He just hasn't figured out how to go about ditching the psycho."

Dillan chuckled.

"Be patient. He'll come around."

Charlie sipped his coffee, lost in thought.

"What about you? What's going on with you and Terr?" Dillan asked.

"We're just friends."

She delivered her best cynical look. "Friends?"

"Well, yeah, at least for now. She's heartbroken over that asshole. All I can do now is be there for her."

Dillan nudged his bulging bicep. "So you do have a little-more-than-friendly feelings for her?"

"How could I not? She's amazing."

Dillan smiled to herself thinking she had to share Charlie's sweet words with Terry.

"I'm starving. Want to go get some pancakes…and bacon…. and eggs…"

"Do you really have to ask?" Dillan teased.

"That's my girl. My treat since you let my ass crash here."

"Leave your ass in your pants."

"No promises."

Dillan burst into laughter, grateful for her

lighthearted relationship with Charlie. She needed it now more than ever.

♡

Landi seemed to linger in Dillan's mind all day. She spent most of the afternoon with her family – baking with her mom, joking with her dad and filling Nick in on details he'd missed, all the while thinking of Landi and the special moments they'd recently shared. His words from the night before stuck with her.

'I want to be close to you… I miss you, Di.'

Did he really mean it?

She wondered how things had gone with Beth, wishfully thinking that maybe they hadn't gone so well. Did he break up with her?

Curiosity got the best of Dillan when she decided to stop by his house, just after leaving her parents' house.

She contemplated texting him but decided that a sneak attack was more practical. If Beth's car was there she'd simply drive by. If it was gone, she'd knock. No need to make herself known unless absolutely necessary. It was a good plan.

The sun had just gone down in a purple hued sky as Dillan drove down Landi's street. She spotted his truck sitting alone in the driveway and breathed a "yay!" before parking a house down at the curb. Dillan calmly got out of her car, straightened her posture, made sure her tank top and jeans looked perfect and walked as if she owned the street. Then nerves kicked in. She hesitated while walking along the stone path, at the sight of lights glowing from the house and whilst standing in front of the door.

What are you doing? This is crazy… isn't it?

She knocked anyway. A few minutes later, Landi

answered appearing exhausted. His hair was in disarray, eyes half open and jaw tense. But he was so handsome…

"Hi," she chirped, with a hopeful smile.

"Di…what are you doing here?"

"Yeah, this is stupid, huh?" She turned and walked into the grass, prepared to get out of there.

"Wait."

She glanced back to see him making a gesture for her to go in.

"Come on."

Landi lay on the couch looking casual in a t-shirt and cargo pants while Dillan sat in the loveseat opposite him feeling uncomfortable. She immediately regretted her decision as she looked around sensing tension. Something was off.

"So, what's going on?" Landi asked, not bothering to even look at her.

"I just want to make sure everything's okay. You seemed really stressed this morning."

"I'm fine."

"So, Beth wasn't upset?"

"A little."

She felt like they were back to square one. He was shutting her out, in one of his moods.

"But everything's good?"

He frowned at her. "Yeah, what's with you?"

"Nothing." Dillan shut up real quick. She felt like a moron for showing up to begin with. She'd set herself up for disappointment and was feeling it.

As she looked around the space, she noticed Beth's stuff everywhere. Multiple pairs of shoes by the door, scarves, jackets…

Dillan was suddenly nauseous.

As ridiculous as it was, she felt as though that stuff should have been hers. It brought unexpected tears to her eyes. She stood up.

"I'm going to go," she said.

Landi sat up and eyed her. "What's wrong?"

"Nothing, I really shouldn't have come in the first place."

"I'm sorry," he said. "I'm not in a good mood. I've had a shitty day and I still feel like shit from last night."

As they looked at each other, Dillan wanted so badly to bring up the night before and the moments they shared but everything inside her told her not to.

"Do you remember what you said to me last night?" she blurted. "How you held me and tried to kiss me...again."

He looked her straight in the eye. "Yeah, what about it?"

She was suddenly embarrassed, caught off guard. She felt her face heat and swallowed – hard. "Don't you have any feelings for me at all?"

Landi looked as if he'd been punched in the stomach.

"Do you ever wonder what it could be like if we were together again?"

"Of course I do but it's not going to happen," he said, taking a swig from a beer on the coffee table.

"Why? Because you can't forgive me?"

"No, I can't."

Dillan placed her hands on her hips. "Why not?"

"Because I don't even know why you left me to begin with, Di." The minute the words left his mouth Landi looked remorseful.

It took everything Dillan had not to burst into tears.

She tried to breathe.

"Why are you still holding this over my head?" she asked.

"Because you haven't told me the truth. That's all I ever wanted, Di. Please talk to me – what happened?"

Dillan wanted to fall to the floor and crumble. To give up, be defeated – cry her eyes out. But she couldn't. She had to fight. She had to avoid the truth as long as she could.

"Do you love Beth?" she asked.

"In my own way, yes. Where is all of this coming from, anyway? I thought we were working on being friends?"

She ignored him, too pissed to listen to his ridiculous reasoning. Friends? What a bunch of BS. "So you're madly in love with her and you're going to marry her?"

"I'm safe with her!"

"That's the stupidest thing I've ever heard!" she yelled. "You're willing to be unhappy for the rest of your life because you don't want to risk getting hurt?"

"Yep."

Dillan was beyond frustrated. She gathered her purse and readied to leave allowing a tiny bit of emotion to overpower her. Tears burst from her eyes.

Landi immediately softened. "Di?"

"I'm so sorry," she cried, wiping tears away. "I'm sorry you've been hurt so bad and I'm sorry that I hurt you. It's not fair. I wish I could just take it all away, but I can't."

Before any more emotion or words could escape, Dillan rushed to the door.

Landi followed, pulling her into a tight embrace before she could get any further. She sobbed in his chest, feeling vulnerable, ashamed and humiliated.

"I feel so stupid," she cried, hating the way her muffled voice sounded in his soft shirt.

"Don't. There's no reason to. I'm here for you, Di, as a friend. We're good at that."

She broke away from her Landi burrow and stared up into his eyes as he wiped tears away.

"Don't cry, it makes me so sad."

But that's all she could do as she took in his caring gaze.

Too little, too late.

Dillan found strength and pulled herself together enough to convince Landi that she was fine enough to be on her way.

The minute she turned off of Tenth Street she pulled the car over and bawled until she couldn't breathe.

Bitch ♡

Dillan? Where are you? Please talk to me.

"Landi, are you listening to me?"

Beth's voice was background noise. The television was much more vivid. Swarms of color melted into one as Landi's thoughts brought him back to the nagging guilt in the pit of his gut. No matter how hard he tried, it wouldn't go away.

He was glad to have had an insanely busy work week that left him exhausted and unable to do anything other than sleep, eat and get up to work again. The only person he made a point to see was his mom – and of course he'd texted Dillan a few times with no response.

He was worried.

Afraid he'd damaged their newfound friendship or worse – hurt her. All he could do was wait to see if she'd come around. In the meantime the silence was killing him.

"Landi!"

Beth's face came into view as she straddled him on the couch. It was impossible to ignore her now.

"Sorry, what?"

"I said, we should go on a romantic getaway like Nick and Erika. They're going to Vegas in a few weeks – what are we going to do?"

"I can't take time off for something like that right now."

Beth pushed her bottom lip out. It only annoyed him.

"Plus, I can't leave my mom. If something happened…"

"Can't we go *somewhere*? Maybe the coast?"

Irritation soared. Landi shoved her off of his lap and stood, walking to the kitchen to get a glass of water. He stared out at the dark window watching rain droplets slide down the pane.

"Landi? What is with you?" Beth was at his side, now angry.

He turned to look at her, scanning her oval face, large eyes, small nose and full lips. Her attractiveness was appealing. But what was behind the façade?

"Why do you love me?" he asked, catching her off guard.

"What do you mean?"

"Why?"

She bit her lip, smiled, laughed, looked away then sighed and raised an eyebrow at him.

"I think you know exactly why…" she said, running a hand over his chest.

Landi stepped back. "I'm serious, Beth. What do we have in common? What connects us?"

"Everything."

In that moment Landi saw a small, lost girl before him scrambling for the right answer.

"Are we going to Charlie's party this weekend?"

she asked, completely missing the point of the conversation.

Landi felt as if a brick had been thrown at his stomach.

"I'm planning on it," was all he could manage as he sipped water. He was dying to see Dillan.

"Is *she* going to be there?"

"Most likely."

"Well, I should probably go to make sure that bitch doesn't try to steal you away."

"Seriously? You're the one who's the bitch," he snapped.

Beth's face turned bright red. She raised her hand giving Landi a hint of exactly what he was getting. He clenched his jaw as she delivered a mean slap with a force he didn't know she possessed.

He stared at the grains in the wood floor waiting for the sting to dissipate.

"Fuck you! I'm out of here." She rushed out of the kitchen to the front door. Landi followed. He watched as she fumbled to get her designer shoes on.

"Beth, I'm sorry. I shouldn't have said that..."

"Screw you!"

"I can't do this anymore."

"What do you mean, *this*?" she snapped.

"Us, you and me, I'm done..."

"Don't you *dare*. I don't want to hear any more shit from you!"

She stomped her foot into her shoes and grabbed her purse, giving Landi one last snarl before turning to walk out the door.

He watched her leave without an attempt to make her stay.

He'd never been so glad to be alone.

Blind Date ♡

Dillan stared at her cell phone with an emptiness she'd hoped to never feel again. Only, it was all she could feel since Landi had made it clear he wanted nothing to do with her. Her heart ached terribly.

She nestled into her blanket cocoon on the couch contemplating whether or not to answer Landi's pleas. Even three consecutive evenings of her most comfortable pajamas, fluffy slippers and re-runs couldn't shake her mood.

"I'm here for you, Di, as a friend..."

The most depressing thing she'd ever heard. She didn't want to be *just* friends. That realization was crushing. But the idea of living the rest of her life without her true love was devastating.

`If you don't respond I'm coming to find you. I'm worried.`

That got her attention. The question was, did she want him there? Absolutely.

Dillan jumped from her sadness crater straight to

the bathroom. A hot shower, fresh shave and clean underwear were in order. Nothing wrong with being prepared – just in case.

But as she slathered shaving cream over her thighs reality hit – hard. What the hell was she doing? A booty call was the last thing they needed... even though her body craved his so very badly.

Half covered in soap and cream Dillan wrapped herself in a towel and rushed back to the living room where her phone sat on the arm of the couch.

`I'm fine. I just need space.`

Tears sprang from her eyes the minute she hit the send button.

Then the doorbell rang.

"Shit! Shit..." Dillan wiped her face, flung her hair back and ran to the front door in nothing but her striped beach towel.

"Who is it?" she yelled.

"Guess?"

She opened the door to see two sets of wide eyes – one brown and one blue. Tyann eyed her towel. Terry gave a wry smile. No need for a panic attack.

"What's going on in here?" Terry asked, eyeing the space behind her as if to find something kinky.

She rolled her eyes. "A whole lot of nothing. Me, showering and being depressed."

"Well, we need to change that." Tyann walked right to Dillan's comfy spot on the couch and wrapped herself in the down comforter. Terry joined her, stealing her own blanket half.

Dillan chuckled at her friends before heading back to the shower to finish rinsing. She returned wearing fleece pants and an oversized sweatshirt to find Tyann and Terry in a television coma. She joined them underneath the white poof. It was a Tyann, Dillan and Terry sandwich.

"Are you okay?" Tyann asked, turning her attention to Dillan.

"No," she admitted, hating the way it sounded out loud. She filled them in on the details regarding her latest text and decision not to make that booty call.

"He loves you so damned much," Terry stated. "It's blatantly obvious. I don't know what his problem is… other than the fact that he's a male."

"I can't believe he's letting the past get in the way of your future," Tyann said. "That's such bullshit."

"He's scared. He doesn't want to risk anything," Dillan added.

"And you can't wait for him to snap out of it!" Terry snapped her fingers for effect.

"Exactly. Which is why you're moving on," Tyann said.

"I am?"

"Yes. You need a fresh start. We need to find you a man."

"I don't want a man, I hate men!"

"So did I." Terry's glossy pink lips grinning at her made Dillan laugh.

"Oh God, how's your whole dilemma?"

"I'm done with Jesse."

"You're done?" Dillan sounded a little surprised.

"Done. Unless he can completely change and prove to me that he's a different person and that he would never ever do anything like that again."

"Good for you."

"And in the meantime I've got Charlie, which, as a bonus, drives Jesse crazy."

Dillan laughed.

"Yeah, be careful with that," Tyann remarked.

"With what?" Terry asked, looking offended.

"Charlie."

"He's harmless," Dillan added.

Tyann raised an eyebrow. "Since when?"

Dillan answered with a sly, knowing grin. She knew the truth. Charlie had spilled his heart out to her over breakfast the other day.

"Anyway, where should we go?" Terry asked, standing as if getting ready to bolt. "We definitely need to change and…"

"I don't want to go anywhere," Dillan said, pulling the blanket up to her chin. "Will you guys just stay here and hang out with me?"

Tyann gave her a hug. "Of course. We're here for you."

The three snuggled on the couch in comfy clothes watching cheesy shows while snacking and talking. Dillan was thankful for her girlfriends and the support they offered when she needed it most. Their boost gave her the strength she needed to let go, move on and allow things to be. She didn't want to hurt Landi, Beth or herself anymore.

♡

"I have a proposition for you."

Dillan suspiciously eyed Tyann from across the table they shared at Francine's Mexican Restaurant. She wasn't sure she'd ever heard that word come out of her best friend's mouth. "Okay?"

"When you're ready, if you want, I know a really sweet, good looking, single guy I thought you might be interested in…"

"All right, stop there. When I said I was ready to move on I didn't mean two days later with a stranger."

It had only been a couple of days since their girl night in. Dillan was a bit shocked that Tyann was already trying to hook her up. She sipped her raspberry lemonade wishing it was a full-blown margarita. Damned lunch hour.

"I'm sorry. I shouldn't have brought it up." Tyann stared down at the table.

Dillan sighed. "Who is it?"

She perked right back up. "I work with him."

"He's a teacher?"

"Yeah, an incredible one."

Dillan tried not to roll her eyes again. "Well, if he's so great, why doesn't he have a girlfriend?"

"Just got out of a serious relationship six months ago."

"Uh, I don't know..."

"Trust me, he's over her." Tyann adjusted her bright purple halter-top.

"And you know because?"

"The guy's a really good friend. I would never set you up with a jerk, or a stranger."

"I don't know, Ty."

"Why don't you come out with us tonight and meet him?" Tyann's excitement made it difficult to say no, even though Dillan wanted to more than anything. "I'll ask Terry and Charlie to come so it'll be a group thing and not an official date."

Dillan took a long sip of her lemonade. If she choked on her drink would it suffice for an answer?

"Come on, Di. I'm not asking you to marry him." Tyann tapped her freshly manicured nails on the table.

"Fine. But if I'm not into him I'm leaving."

"Deal. I'll call you later with details."

Oh joy.

Dillan I'm sorry. Please don't ignore me. I care about you so much.

She sat in her car in the parking lot of Swanky's wanting to turn around and go right back home. Landi's text, the sudden rainstorm and darkness of night made her feel even more depressed.

Damn you, Tyann.

Dillan: Truce?

Landi: Truce ☺

Clearing things up with Landi made her feel better but she still didn't want to meet what's-his-face. She didn't even try to look good. Work makeup, jeans and a girl t-shirt. Woo hoo.

She sat in her car for nearly ten minutes trying to persuade herself to go in when Charlie and Terry pulled up beside her looking amped. Terry was dressed in a short black mini dress and five inch heels and Charlie looked hot in a muscle accentuating shirt, jeans and his signature hat turned backwards. They practically dragged her in and instantaneously set a drink in front of her, but she just wasn't in the mood.

"What's the matter, Di?" Terry asked.

I miss Landi. But she couldn't say it out loud.

"I'm tired."

"Wake up, girl! It's party time!" Charlie did a silly dance making her laugh.

Tyann and Jason joined them just in time for a huge pitcher of beer. Tyann was in an even tighter mini dress than Terry and Jason was looking like his usual classy self in a button down shirt and stylish jeans. Dillan received hugs and kisses from Tyann and Terry. Charlie and Jason talked amongst themselves while the girls huddled around the table.

"I don't think he's here yet," Tyann said, looking around the dimly lit room. "You're going to like him." She glanced at Dillan. Her smile instantly faded. "At least try to act a little excited."

Dillan looked at her friend with sad eyes as Tyann shoved her drink in front of her.

"Don't think about him. Drink this."

"But..."

"Just do it."

Halfway into Dillan's story about Landi's depressing attempts to contact her and their semi-make-up texting, Tyann's eyes grew huge. She flashed her phone is Dillan's face temporarily blinding her.

"He'll be here in a minute!"

Dillan didn't share her excitement. "I'm going to go freshen up."

As Dillan fought her way through a sweaty crowd of partygoers, fog and blinding laser lights, she seriously considered slipping out the back door when a familiar voice caught her attention.

"Dillan Coggwell? Is that you?"

She turned to see intense green eyes and a sweet, genuine smile.

"Emmett? Holy shit!"

She hugged her long-lost friend, overjoyed to see him. Emmett and Dillan had been good friends all throughout high school, having interest in the same studies and sharing most academic classes. They'd always had an attraction to one another but set any feelings aside because of their deep relationships with other partners.

"What are you doing here?" he asked, eyeing her figure.

Dillan couldn't help but do the same. Emmett was tall with a lean, muscular build, had short, disheveled dirty blonde hair and a good sense of style. He'd always been smart, fun and dedicated to his future. Dillan suddenly wasn't feeling so bad.

"I just moved back."

His smile had her mesmerized. "Seriously? Shit, we have to catch up."

"Are you here with someone?" she asked.

"No, just my friends."

"Buy me a drink?"

"Hell, yes."

Dillan reintroduced Emmett to a not-so-happy Tyann and Terry who were hanging out with an unfamiliar guy – the blind date. Dillan politely introduced herself to the stranger as she and Emmett joined them for conversation. After a couple drinks, Dillan whisked Emmett to a private spot. She couldn't wait to see what her old friend had been up to.

Partygoers ♡

"What do you mean, she's seeing someone?"

Landi couldn't ignore the gaping pit that tore through his gut.

"Dillan's bringing a date to the party," Jason said, grabbing another case of beer from the liquor store cooler. He and Landi walked through the aisles in flip flops, t-shirts, shorts and his flannel of course, grabbing beverages to bring to Charlie's shindig.

"Seriously? Who?"

"I don't know. Some guy she met at a bar."

Wow. I'm that easily replaced?

"Don't flip out," Jason warned, giving him a stern glance.

"I'm not going to. I'm happy for her."

"Yeah, well...maybe you should tell Beth to come."

"About that..."

Jason stopped in the middle of the wine aisle. "What?"

"I don't even know if we're together anymore. I tried to break it off with her after I called her a bitch."

Jason attempted to hold back a laugh but failed. "Sorry."

"She hasn't contacted me since."

"Unless she blatantly and clearly confirmed that you are indeed broken up assume that you're not," he continued to the spirits sections grabbing a few more bottles. "Especially when it comes to that piece of work."

Landi couldn't concentrate on anything other than the pain that clawed at his soul. He tried to ignore it, talk himself out of it, think about anything else but all that kept surfacing was a vision of Dillan with another man.

It bugged the shit out of him.

Charlie's parents house was already surrounded by vehicles and people happily skipping inside as the sun began to set behind the hills. It reminded him of high school. Charlie's house was *the* party place when they were teens. He and Dillan always enjoyed making out on the trampoline in the backyard… he and Dillan.

Landi took a deep breath, tore into a case of beer and downed a can before getting out of Jason's car.

"Whoa, dude. Slow down. We've got all night…" Jason raised a suspicious eyebrow at him. "Are you sure you're okay?"

"Fan fucking tastic."

Jason didn't look convinced.

They walked in the back gate with armfuls of party goods greeted by Nick, Erika, Tyann, Terry and of course Charlie who was filling two large coolers with beer.

No Dillan.

Landi decided to make himself useful by busying himself with whatever he could in order not to think. And being around mountainfulls of beer was a plus. He tended to the coolers and the food, then started a fire in the backyard pit, already feeling stress melt off his shoulders.

Music blared throughout the crisp evening air as friends danced, drank and laughed the night away. Jason pulled Landi to a table where he, Charlie, Nick and a few other guys were seated watching the girls dance in the glow of tiny white lights strung throughout the backyard.

"Where is she?" he heard himself ask aloud.

Jason grinned at him. "I don't know but you should probably slow down on the beer."

He had a point. No need to make an ass out of himself. He needed to be sharp this evening. Stay alert. Be observant. See what was *really* going on.

Landi went inside to take a piss and get some water when his pocket buzzed. It was Beth.

We need to talk. I miss you.

It was a hook to reel him back in. A desperate attempt to keep him under her control. He hadn't heard a drop from her since their fight. What a convenient reminder.

Landi turned his phone off and joined the guys back at the patio table.

Nick got out a joint, lit it up and passed it around. Landi's stomach sank. The smell, look and concept of smoking pot still bothered him even after years of sobriety. He'd nearly lost everything at such a young age because of it. Including Dillan. The memories were too much. He was about to leave the table when Jason pointed toward the gate entrance.

Nothing could hamper the adrenaline that surged through Landi's veins seeing Dillan hand in hand with a guy who looked eerily familiar. She was gorgeous – smiling with glossy lips, hair in an up-do, dark smoky eyeliner, a classy, yet revealing top that accented her breasts perfectly, legs that could kill…

Awareness hit him unexpectedly.

He watched her giggle and gossip as Emmett stood by. Within a few minutes she was heading his way, dragging her puppy along. When they caught eyes, Dillan smiled, though apprehension was evident. She was nervous.

"Hey, Landi," she chimed.

"Hi."

"This is Emmett."

Emmett…something about the guy was ridiculously familiar. Emmett held his hand out. Landi glared at him. He immediately backed away.

Message delivered.

"Be nice!" Tyann yelled, slapping Landi on the shoulder as soon as Dillan and Emmett were out of earshot. Nick burst out laughing.

"That was fucking hilarious!" he yelled, a little too loudly. He was high as a kite.

Landi kept a sharp eye on Dillan and Emmett as they mingled throughout the party. He was on high alert, waiting, watching – ready to act. On what, he wasn't sure. But it seemed of utmost importance. He was on a mission. A mission to ensure Dillan's safety and well being. He was her soldier and he'd march to the end of the earth for her.

Of course the buzz he'd caught earlier only intensified the feelings roiling through his body.

Jason appeared beside Landi as he slowly sipped a beer on the patio steps watching Dillan.

"Are you all right?" he asked.

"Yep."

"You wanna go for a walk or something? Tyann

wants to check out the neighborhood."

"No."

"Landi!"

For the first time he looked at Jason. There was deep concern in his ice blue eyes.

"Stop, man. You're only making this harder for yourself."

"I can't help it. I have to make sure she's okay."

"She's fine, dude. Maybe we should get out of here? We could go catch a movie or swim at my house…"

"Who is that guy?" Landi interrupted.

"Emmett…Emmett Day? You don't remember him? The guy from high school…"

He looked back to where Dillan and Emmett were now dancing under the tiny white lights. The realization hit him like a smack to the face. Emmett Day – the asshole who was always hitting on his girlfriend all throughout high school. That guy.

Anger flamed, boiled and gnarled its way through Landi's body. He could feel his hands shake, face prickle, heart race.

"Landi?"

He watched as they stared into each other's eyes, laughed, teased, touched. When Emmett's hands landed on Dillan's hips, something broke inside of Landi.

So many emotions bubbled up he wasn't sure which one to grasp. All he knew was that he didn't want that guy – or any guy – touching her.

"Fuck!"

Blind rage carried him into the mob of people surrounding them and right up to Emmett. He pushed him with a force he didn't know he had causing Emmett to land in the grass so hard he actually skidded.

Landi heard yelling and gasps but couldn't focus on anything other than Emmett staring up at him in confusion.

"Don't you ever fucking touch her again!" Landi yelled. "If you so much as look at her I will fucking kill you! Do you understand? DO YOU UNDERSTAND?"

"Yesss…" Emmett managed, frozen in fear on the ground.

Multiple hands pulled at Landi. He shrugged them off and stormed out the back gate into the streets.

Tears wet his face as he disappeared into the darkness.

Friends? ♡

"**D**id you tell him about your "surfing" accident?" Tyann asked, just as dumbfounded by Landi's sudden attack as Dillan was.   "No," she cried, still trying to comprehend what had happened.

Emmett stood up attempting to brush the grass off of himself. He had stains all up his back.

Dillan wasn't sure what to do or say.   "I'm so sorry…"

"I'm going to go," he said. And that was that. Emmett was gone.

Dillan felt bad but all she could think of was Landi. She worried about him being alone, inebriated and hurt in the streets.

If he was feeling half of what Dillan felt after she'd seen him and Beth together, he'd be a wreck. His reaction was proof enough.

"Well, someone must have told him something," Tyann insisted, still looking panicked.

"He's just being protective. I know exactly how he

feels."

"Holy shit, are you okay?" Nick asked, running over to his sister with an overly amused expression. He chuckled to himself, obviously high.

"I need to find him."

"Don't look at me," Nick said. "I'm fucked the fuck up."

Dillan struggled to pull her phone out of her skintight jeans. Her hands shook.

I'm not mad. Call me. Now.

She felt helpless. All she wanted was to make Landi feel better. To talk things through. Explain, work things out. Like friends do. Nothing else mattered.

She grabbed her purse from the back bedroom, readying to leave if need be. Tyann stopped her on her way back through the hallway.

"Jason and Charlie went on a walk to find him," she said. "Don't worry, he'll be back."

But all she could do was worry. There was no way she could just stand around and wait.

"Let's go too. Come with me, Ty."

"No, we don't need to be walking around in the dark. I promise they'll find him. Let's go inside and relax."

"I can't just sit around and wait." Dillan was ready to make a run for it when her phone lit up.

Meet me at THE park. You know where.

Dillan managed to get away from her protective friend. She ran down Parker Street in five-inch heels, skinny jeans and a flouncy club top. She couldn't help but feel a smidgen like a hooker running through the upper class neighborhood – her boobs happily bouncing along. The air was electric with a crisp dewy scent. Sprinklers misted on the lawns as Dillan passed beautifully lit-up

172

homes. She couldn't wait to get to her man.

Once at the ball field, Dillan took off her shoes and walked barefoot through water drenched lawn, past the cement walking path and through huge cottonwoods beside a gurgling creek that led to the spot where Landi was waiting beneath the stars. She immediately recognized his shadow sitting upon the enormous log that extended directly over the creek lit up by moonlight. Dillan couldn't help but smile.

Without words, Landi met her, grabbed her hand and led her safely to the middle of the log where they sat side by side. It was hard to see much of anything in the dark but Dillan could still make out Landi's adorable face. She knew he'd been crying.

"You remembered," he said.

She smiled. "Of course I do. We've only met here about a thousand times. Why? Were you testing me?"

"No." He laughed.

Dillan was glad to get a chuckle out of him. She turned to admire his profile as he looked at the water below.

"That was pretty extreme, wasn't it?" he said.

"A little. But I understand why you did it."

"At least it wasn't as bad as Charlie and Jesse's brawl."

They gave each other a silly grin.

"Why Emmett? Of all people. I hate that asshole," Landi said staring deeply into her eyes.

"You never gave him a chance – now or then."

"Yeah, well. I don't think it really matters who it is. If they're interested in you I don't like them."

Dillan was flattered. She swung her legs back and forth. "We have to find a way to get over our feelings for one another."

"We do?"

She laughed. "Why are you so surprised? We're supposed to be friends, remember?"

"Oh, yeah."

They gave each other the classic Dillan and Landi smile – the one nobody else understood.

A pocket of cold air drifted from the water causing Dillan to shiver. Without even a flinch Landi removed his flannel and wrapped it around her shoulders. Tingles erupted. He was still the sweet, chivalrous boy she'd fallen in love with.

"I'm sorry I've been distant," Dillan said, snuggling into his warm shirt. "I thought it was best to have a little space."

"I don't want any space between us," he said, catching her gaze with a passionate look of his own. He eyed her lips.

"I want to kiss you so bad."

Dillan was breathless. She couldn't help but giggle. "How bad?"

"Ridiculously."

"How many times have we kissed on this log?" she asked, enjoying teasing him.

Landi laughed. "I don't know. At least one-hundred."

"Let's make it one hundred and one." Dillan leaned in and planted a smooch on him and got a passionate, mind-blowing kiss in return. Their mouths working together in a perfect dance as if they'd never been apart. Sparks exploded and burst into flames. Dillan was knocked stupid by the endorphins running through her body. She knew Landi felt the same as he looked at her with a dazed expression.

"Holy shit."

Dillan laughed, feeling lovesick all over again.

"We better get off of this log before I fall on my ass."

"I won't let you fall," Dillan said, grabbing his hand.

He gave her a loving smile. "What do you want to do?"

"Go somewhere warm."

"I don't have a car."

"Me either."

They burst into laughter.

"Our parent's houses are the closest," Dillan said, pointing down the creek. The routes they used to take as kids were coming back.

"Good plan."

Dillan and Landi walked hand in hand toward Jan's home in the park listening to the crickets chirp and the water trickle. There was nowhere in the world Dillan would rather be. Halfway there she received a piggyback ride as they laughed and goofed off all the way to Jan's back door. They stood on the dark patio shushing each other as Landi looked for the extra key under rocks and crevices.

"Found it," he whispered, holding it up.

Dillan watched him unlock and open the door thinking how cute he looked. She wanted so badly to follow him in but knew what it would lead to. Her inner teen wanted to fall back in love with Landi and make sweet love to him. But the adult was afraid, protective – a party pooper.

"Okay, I've got to go wake up my parents now," she said with a fake smile.

"What?" Landi's tone and frown expressed pure hurt. "Don't leave."

"It's bad enough that you're breaking in to your own mother's house – I don't want to get in trouble, too."

"Breaking in?" he said.

"You know what I mean."

"No, I don't." He grabbed her hand and slowly pulled her through the sliding glass door with him. The house was warm, dark and quiet. Landi closed the door then looked at Dillan and tucked a stray hair behind her ear. She stared up into his adoring eyes.

"You really don't want to stay?" he whispered.

"Of course I do," she said. "But you know what will happen if I do."

He smiled. "Uh, sleep? Maybe snuggling."

"That's a great plan but I'm not sure I can stick to it."

The grin that appeared on Landi's face was devilishly handsome. "I'm okay with that."

Dillan's heart couldn't refuse. "Don't say I didn't warn you…friend."

Stumbling through Jan's house at midnight brought back comical memories and a giddiness that effected Dillan and Landi as they shushed each other in the dark. He led her to his old room where they shut the door and turned on a dim bedside lamp. They giggled at each other in the orange glow.

"This is really weird," Landi said. "In a good way."

Dillan tossed her shoes and purse down and immediately began rummaging for makeshift comfy clothes.

"Look in the closet," Landi said, knowing exactly what she was doing. He removed his shirt and shorts then got into the vintage twin sized bed as Dillan found a favorite Landi t-shirt.

"I'm stealing this, by the way," she said, happily removing her tight jeans and top in front of him. She was glad to have her lacy black strapless bra and matching underwear on.

Landi's jaw dropped causing her to burst into laughter.

"Like you haven't seen it a million times."

"It gets better every time."

Dillan jumped onto the bed in her oversized shirt and underwear. The act was all so familiar. They tangled themselves up in each other beneath the blankets, noses, feet, arms, legs entwined as they stared into each other's eyes. It was perfectly natural. Landi gently caressed the hair at her temple, causing goose bumps.

"You're so amazing."

Dillan answered with a seductive kiss pressing every inch of her body into his. She was hungry for his love, feeling an ache stir deep within. Her heart raced as his hands searched her curves with slow, deliberate strokes finding her hips, thighs, stomach and breasts. His touch alone had her out of breath as their tongues danced. She grazed his chest with light strokes and teased him with a finger just inside the band of his boxers. He gave a soft moan as she broke the kiss and gazed into Landi's heavy lidded eyes. She saw a longing she'd missed. He knew exactly what was going on inside of her – and precisely how to intensify it.

Dillan's ache turned into a raging need. Overwhelming feelings and emotions flooded her senses. Landi slowly removed her shirt, bra and panties taking his time planting soft kisses and nibbles. She was caught in a whirlwind of desire, lost in a world she had forgotten about until now. She closed her eyes and quietly whimpered feeling Landi's rock hard erection against her hips.

Landi trailed her body with nips and kisses. He took a second to stare at her naked figure before teasing and taunting her breasts, nearly pushing her over the edge. All she could think of was how he would feel inside of her now, three years later. Her body yearned for him, needing him more than ever.

She tried to pull him closer but he traced kisses down her stomach to her sweet spot. When his tongue reached between her thighs she thought she would die. Dillan clawed at the sheets trying desperately not to wake Ms. Powell. It wouldn't be the first time.

Landi teased her until she was on the brink, then pulled the blankets around them, wrapping their naked bodies together in a cocoon of fabric. They kissed with all the love and passion they had for each other, taking a moment to soak it all in. As they silently bonded, Landi gave her exactly what she wanted. Their bodies rocked in an ocean of pleasure until they were breathless and spent, full of each other's love. After tender kisses and sweaty snuggles, Dillan fell fast asleep wrapped up in Landi's arms. In that moment, it felt like they'd never been apart.

Crazies ♡

Landi stirred, feeling a body perfectly cradled into his. His sweet Dillan. He turned to hold her and breathe in the tantalizing scent of her hair. He couldn't resist opening his eyes to see a beautiful angel sound asleep in the soft glow of morning light coming from the window. Her blonde waves were tossed around the pillow and over his shoulder reminding him of the countless times he'd watched her sleep thinking she was perfect.

As he lingered in admiration, she nestled even closer to him, nuzzling her nose into his neck.

"I love you, Dillan," he whispered, liking the way it sounded out loud. It had been way too long since he'd meant those three words.

She kissed his neck and ran a hand through his hair, creating instant desire. No girl had ever affected him the way she did.

Ever.

He was more than ready to make love to her all over again when a strange sound erupted.

Whispers?

Landi looked at his door to see it open a crack. Faint commotion came from the hall. Then his mom appeared. She grinned...and waved. Landi didn't think he'd ever been more mortified. Oh, wait. He had. Courtesy of his dear mom.

"Hi honey," she said, actually walking into the room in her robe and slippers. "Would you and Di like some coffee?"

"I'd like some privacy, Mom."

"I'm sorry. I'm just so excited! Linda and I were just going to start breakfast..."

"You and Linda? Really?"

A muffled laugh came from Dillan who was still buried in his neck.

"Oh, we've been talking about you two all morning. Come and join us when you're ready."

Landi watched Jan exit and facepalmed himself. "Remind me to never crash at my mom's house ever again."

He and Dillan busted up laughing, which turned into silliness, and kissing. He ran a hand over her thigh, feeling a slight difference in the skin texture. Her scar. His stomach immediately tightened.

"Are you ever going to tell me about this?" he asked, at risk of shifting the mood.

She pulled his fingers away from her thigh to her lips and gently kissed his fingers.

"I hope I can someday. I want to but I'm scared."

"Of what?"

"Hurting you."

The fact that she cared so much about him meant more than he could express. "But *you* were hurt, right?"

180

She swallowed and looked away, then nodded. It killed him. He didn't want to acknowledge the twist of intense emotions that were stirred up by the thought. Instead, he held her close and kissed away any tension.

"Thank you," she said.

"For what?"

"For this. For reminding me of what it feels like to love, and be loved."

Tears rimmed his eyes. "You don't have to thank me, sweetheart."

"I know. But I want to."

He smiled, loving her even more.

"I don't want you to feel like you have to do something drastic just because we slept together," she said.

He arched an eyebrow. "Like what?"

"Like breaking up with Beth."

"What if I want to?"

"Then go for it. This is all your fault anyway, remember…friend?"

"Smartass…"

They kissed, lost in a Landi and Dillan world all over again until Linda and Jan's chatter interrupted their make-out session.

"Should we go join the crazies?" Dillan asked, poking Landi's chin.

"I guess we should get it over with."

"Let's pretend like we hate each other. They'll be so caught off guard."

Landi laughed at how cute she was. "You're a troublemaker."

"You know it," Dillan said with a wink, causing his heart to flutter.

♡

Beth: Why are you ignoring me? Meet me at the house later. You better be there.

♡

Landi looked up into the bright summer sun feeling its rays sink into his entire being. He couldn't remember the last time he felt so alive, present – happy. But the sun had nothing to do with it. Dillan was responsible for the warmth radiating from his being. For once, everything felt right.

"I haven't seen you like this since we were kids," Jason said, grinning at him from across the park picnic table. His sunglasses and spiked hair reminded Landi of the teen Jason. "It's like we've been transported back to high school with you and Di together again. It's awesome."

"She's the one. She always has been."

"I could have told you that."

They broke into laughter while they watched their women swing in the playground with Nick standing by to tease them. Landi's heart skipped when Dillan smiled at him. The sound of lawnmowers, sprinklers and children's laughter echoed through the air.

"What are you going to do about Beth?" Jason asked.

"Officially break up with her and marry the love of my life."

"At least she has a clue that it's coming. Erika probably told her everything that she witnessed last night, too."

A pit formed in Landi's stomach just thinking about Beth's negativity. "I don't care. I'm done. I'm breaking it off tonight."

He admired the way Dillan's hair tousled from the swing's momentum, contrasting with the calm blue sky. Nick tickled her every time she swung forward in his direction. Landi found her giggles and protests amusing.

"Let me know if you need a place to stay," Jason said, bringing Landi's thoughts back to the picnic table. "Beth can be a handful."

"It'll be fine. I'm just going to have a calm, adult conversation with her, give her a day to get her crap out and rip the band-aid off as quickly as possible."

"Calm?" Jason smirked. "Adult? Those words and Beth don't go together."

"She's just going to have to deal with it. I'm not buying into her drama."

Landi didn't want to think about Beth or the time he'd wasted with her. All that mattered was Dillan and their bright future.

"What are you guys talking about?" Dillan asked, joining them at the table. She pulled Landi in for a kiss before he could even respond. The scent of her hair, softness of her lips and overwhelming presence overrode any thoughts that were currently forming.

"I don't remember," he managed, causing Jason to chuckle.

Dillan nestled into him as he put his arms around her, holding her as close as possible. They kissed and nuzzled in their own universe until Dillan stood and pulled on his arm.

"Come play with me."

The thoughts that came to Landi's mind were X-rated. She smirked. "In the playground... dork."

Only Dillan could have him climbing over nets, under monkey bars and making out on slides. It didn't matter what they did as long as they were together. They wrestled like lovers as their friends watched on – thoroughly entertained.

When the sun went down, it was nearly impossible for Landi to leave Dillan's townhome. They'd been doing nothing but soaking in each other's love –

 making out in every room, eating, having tickle fights, watching television, poking and teasing one another. Landi promised Dillan a thousand times he'd call or text her and after at least a million kisses and a trillion hugs he reluctantly got into his pick-up truck and headed to Tenth Street.

Cheerios ♡

Maybe she should have been, but Dillan wasn't the least bit surprised to see Terry flushed, confused and a little disoriented after her late-night meeting with Jesse.

She walked into Dillan's townhome startling Tibby and Dillan who were content on the living room floor in their pajamas – Dillan in Landi's t-shirt; Tibby in her coordinating princess set – counting, eating and stacking cheerios.

"Mommy, Mommy, Mommy!" Little Tibby ran to Terry who wore heels and a skirt. She struggled to pick up her daughter, wobbling like a person on stilts.

"Hi, sweetie."

Dillan watched as the two smiled and giggled at each other. There was pure love between them; there was no doubt about that. Dillan felt a twinge of envy wondering if she would share the same bond with her own child someday.

Terry was dragged over to the Cheerio kingdom on the floor. Tibby enthusiastically showed her mother her work and got excited all over again. Terry gave Dillan a wry smile.

"So?" Dillan inquired, already guessing there was drama involved.

"You don't want to know."

"Oh, yes I do."

Terry sighed and ran a hand through her wavy auburn locks before joining them on the floor. She removed her heels and threw her hair up in a messy bun. "Bear with me, I'm still trying to process."

"Oh, goodness." Dillan waited, curiosity eating at her while she munched on Cheerios.

"Well, it wasn't exactly a pleasant meal. We were at each other's throats the whole time and I practically cross-examined him with twenty questions, well, more like one hundred questions. But I got some answers."

She sighed, and then squeezed out a smile for Tibby.

"Her name is Emily. He met her at work and started seeing her four months before we split. He supposedly broke it off with her as of the night I found out... and get this – she's seventeen!"

"What?" Dillan wasn't too surprised considering she'd already seen Miss Teen.

Tears welled up Terry's blue eyes. "I have to say though, in a way it makes me feel better, at least I'm not competing with another woman. She's a girl for Christ's sake!"

"Terr..." Dillan warned, reminding her of Tibby's watchful eyes.

Terry stiffened, attempting to compose herself. She tickled Tibbs to break the tension.

"What else did he have to say?" Dillan asked.

"He told me how important Tibby and I are to him and that he wants us back, then we got to talking about Charlie and that's what set us off again."

"Uh, oh."

"I ended up throwlng my water at him and the next thing I know we're in the women's restroom going at it in a stall."

Dillan gasped. If she hadn't swallowed that last Cheerio she'd be choking on it. "Terry!"

"I know." She looked at the floor.

"I'm confused. Is everything good now or..."

"Not even close. I slapped him and got the hell out of there."

Dillan busted up laughing making Tibby laugh with her. She was thankful that Tibbs had no clue what they were talking about.

"Silly Mommy."

"Silly Goose." Terry beamed at her daughter then kissed the top of her head.

As soon as Dillan caught her breath, she gave her friend sympathetic eyes. Thoughts of Jesse and all the hurt he had caused caught up with her.

"So, that's it?" she asked. "What did he have to say for himself? Does he even feel bad about what he's done?"

Terry shrugged. "If he didn't before, he does now. He said he's been trying to break it off with her from the beginning."

"Sure he has," Dillan said, rolling her eyes. She'd heard that story before.

"I don't even know what to think right now. I'm so overwhelmed." Terry lay down on the floor as a bouncy Tibby crawled all over her. Dillan smiled. Terry didn't even seem to notice the human jungle gym she'd been turned into.

"At least you got answers, like you said. No more mysteries. It was probably good for both of you to just get everything out in the open, even if it wasn't in a very civil manner."

Terry looked to her friend with hope. "You think?"

"Yes. He loves you Terr, he's just a stupid, Neanderthal man who thinks with his penis ninety nine percent of the time."

They grinned at one another.

"I'm just not ready to trust him again, it's going to take a long time."

"That's a good thing," Dillan stated. "It's going to be okay."

"Mommy, Mommy, Mommy..." Tibby had progressed to bounced on Terry as if she were galloping on a horse.

Terry gave Dillan a sweet, dreamy smile.

"What?"

"Nothing, I'm just so happy for you and Landi."

Dillan grinned at the fluffy feeling his name conjured. "Me too. I love him so damned much."

Tibby threw a handful of Cheerios in the air while her mother crawled around the floor picking them up. Dillan's head was somewhere in the clouds thinking of Landi.

Abyss ♡

Landi wasn't surprised to see his house dark and empty. He was relieved.

After retrieving his mail and paper he walked up the path to the front door and turned the key, unsure of what to expect.

Maybe she already took all of her crap and left.

Wrong.

There were Beth accessories all over the place – exactly where she'd left them. A sinking feeling hit Landi's gut. Of course it couldn't be easy.

He immediately went to the bedroom closet, pulled out her oversized designer suitcase and began tossing stuff inside the silk lined abyss. He started in the bedroom, then migrated to the living room, closets and kitchen.

An hour later the suitcase was full but her shit was yet to be cleared. Landi grabbed a box from the garage then tackled the bathroom throwing tampons, shampoo and makeup into the cardboard container.

He'd just picked up dirty clothes from off of the floor

when an object in the small garbage can caught his eye.

A slender white plastic wand. He carefully picked it up and examined the window.

Pregnant.

The word knocked Landi breathless. He dropped the test as a painful jolt shot through his core. Dizziness washed over him. He leaned on the counter trying to get his bearings. His entire body shook.

Fuck, fuck, fuck!

He wanted to scream, cry and punch something all at once. Then the front door opened and closed.

Beth stood before him looking puzzled. She was her classic "perfect" self with just the right amount of makeup on, hair in a half braided up-do and clothed in the latest trendy outfit.

"Are you okay? You look sick..."

Landi ignored her words. He picked up the pregnancy test and shoved it in her face. "What is this?"

She grabbed the wand and stared at it, then opened her gloss-tinted mouth but nothing came out.

"How long have you known?" he asked.

"Well...I suspected...for a little while, but..."

Anger shot through his veins. "Why didn't you tell me? Why wouldn't you tell me? Fuck, Beth!"

"I'm sorry, but with the way things are going...you've been so mean to me!"

"I thought we were careful? What happened? You're still on the pill, right?"

"I might have missed a few days..."

Landi sank to the tiled floor and held his head in his hands trying desperately to soak in the reality of the situation. He couldn't breath as thoughts swirled through his chaotic mind.

He wanted to tell Beth the truth – that he didn't love her and wanted nothing to do with their unborn child, but that would be wrong. Very wrong. How could he express himself without sounding like a complete and total dick? Could he still be with Dillan? He hated himself for the situation he'd put himself in. He wanted to scream like an animal.

"Landi?" her voice grated his nerves. "I know you have feelings for Dillan and I know that things haven't been going very well with us but I still love you. I want to be with you. We can work things out and figure this out together, right?"

He looked up from the floor to see pleading, teary eyes. She was fragile.

"I'm going to go for a walk," was all he could manage.

He burst out the door and walked as fast as he could through the dark streets not seeing anything at all. Tears clouded his vision. He should have known that something would get in the way of his happiness. It always did. His only choice was to harden, suck up and do what he had to do. There was no other option. He had to go back to the mundane life he'd settled for – one that didn't include Dillan. Something inside of him died at the realization.

Screwed Up ♡

"**S**omething's wrong. Something's really wrong," Dillan confessed to her best friend on her lunch break. She fumbled with a stack of fabric swatches at her desk completely uninterested in eating. "He's barely texted me in two days and now he wants to meet to talk. Oh, God."

Tyann sighed on the other end. "Well, maybe he's giving Beth some time to move out or…"

"Maybe he decided that he doesn't really love me."

"That's bullshit and you know it. There's got to be some explanation. You'll find out soon."

"Not soon enough."

Dillan wanted to cry – again. She didn't understand how she and Landi could go from being the smitten lovers they were meant to be to nothing within a matter of days. All she knew was that she couldn't wait to see him. Even if it meant her heart breaking into a thousand pieces. If he chose Beth, she'd live with it. Not happily but she'd deal. All she ever wanted for her sweet Landi was for him to be happy. Even if it were at the cost of her own happiness.

"Please call me as soon as you find out. I want

details," Tyann said.

"I will."

Dillan's insides quivered with nerves all day at work as she anticipated her meeting with Landi. She couldn't think straight she was so worked up. She ended up banging her knee twice, tripped over an invisible bump and shredded an important document. She was a wreck.

At six o clock sharp she pulled into Taren Park. He was already there looking sullen and tired, leaning against his truck in the parking lot. He stared down at the asphalt, his hair covering most of his face. He wore his work shirt and shifted his booted feet. Even the clouds had rolled in casting a dreary shadow over the town.

This isn't going to be good.

Falling back on work mode, Dillan set her fears aside and met him with a smile, getting only a smidgen of eye contact.

Seriously?

"What's going on?" Dillan asked.

"Do you want to walk or…"

"No, I want you to tell me what's up."

He swallowed, shifted and avoided her eyes. "Something happened and…I can't, we can't see each other anymore."

"I assumed, but why?"

"It's complicated."

Dillan's hurt turned to anger. She wasn't expecting her rise of passion. Her hands began to shake. She fisted them to try and control the shaking.

"Do you really expect me to buy that? You think I'm just going to get in my car, drive off and accept that you have a complicated situation that has somehow magically turned you into an asshole again?"

He finally looked at her. Damn those deep hazel eyes full of pain.

"Well, I'm NOT!" she yelled, throwing her hands up in the air. "The least you can do is tell me why the fuck you're acting this way."

He sighed and looked back at the asphalt. "Please, Di. I need you to understand, this is hard enough…"

"I understand that something is really wrong!" Tears began to fly from her eyes. Her entire body shook. "At least look at me!"

He did. And she regretted it immediately. Her heart tore in half seeing that he was just as upset as she was.

"I have to be with Beth," he stated.

"So what happened between us meant nothing?"

 "No, it meant everything…"

"Then why? Why, Landi?"

He swallowed hard. "I found out something that's life changing. I have to be there for Beth."

Clarity knocked Dillan in the head for the first time that day. She knew exactly why.

"She's pregnant," she muttered.

Landi's expression went from mournful to shocked within seconds. He frowned, trying to understand. "How did you know?"

This time Dillan shifted…avoided. She looked down at her red flats… then that nifty spot on the ground. Was that a piece of fossilized gum?

"Dillan?"

"Because…" she breathed. "That's the reason I broke up with you all those years ago." She regretted the painful words that fell from her lips.

Landi's face drained of color. "Wha… what?"

"I have to go." She only made it a step before Landi

stopped her. Now they were face to face. She couldn't avoid him even if she wanted to.

"You were pregnant?" he cried. "With my baby?"

Silence.

"Dillan, talk to me."

But she couldn't talk, she could only cry and try to get to her car. She made it as far as opening the door.

"You can't leave me with this, Di!" Landi said. "I already feel terrible as it is."

She spun to face him bubbling with hurt. "I can do whatever the hell I want! It's not like it's going to change anything!"

"You think I want this?" he yelled. "You think I'm happy to have to settle with a loveless relationship and a shitty situation? I don't! I fucking hate it!"

"Yeah? Well so do I! You're not the only one who's affected by all of this."

A silence fell between them. Thunder boomed in the distance.

"Di, please talk to me. I just want you to be real with me."

"There's no point," she said, sitting in the driver's seat. "It's over, we're over and I'm over it!"

She slammed the door, started the engine and put it in reverse, ignoring Landi's pleas. So much for being calm, collected and rational.

Dillan was so heartbroken she could barely breathe as she drove down blurry streets trying not to get into an accident. She couldn't think, see, inhale, exhale or concentrate on anything other than the pain that was eating her alive.

She didn't know what she needed or where to turn so instinct led her to the one place she knew she'd be loved no matter what.

Home.

Linda panicked seeing Dillan enter through the front door in the shape she was in. It was unusual. She gathered her daughter into her arms and led her to the living room couch where Dillan gasped for air, sobbing into her mother's chest.

"My dear sweet daughter. I love you," she said, running gentle hands over Dillan's silky blonde hair. "Tell me what's bothering you."

Once Dillan was able to take in air without sounding like a cow, she told her mother everything – from how perfectly she and Landi had bonded to the recent fight and horrible situation at hand.

"Oh, baby, I'm so sorry."

"Why does this always happen?" she cried, wiping the snot from her puffy nose.

Linda disappeared into the kitchen and came back with a box of tissues, which she handed to Dillan.

"Every time we have a chance at happiness it gets all screwed up! I'm going to be alone forever!"

"No, you're not," Linda's voice was calm and reassuring. "I know you love him but he's not the only male on earth that can make you happy."

"But he's the only one I want."

"Well, then you're going to have to find a way to make it work."

"What do you mean?" Dillan asked in between blowing her nose.

"Everything can be worked out – one way or another. There are always options."

This was a concept Dillan hadn't even thought about. Options…

"No matter what you choose or decide I am always here for you, Dillan. There is nothing you could do that would make me feel any different."

Feeling slightly lighter, Dillan couldn't pass on a joke.

"Even if I run away and join a convent?"

Linda chuckled. "Even then."

"What if I shave my head and pierce my face?"

"That would be a little scary, but I'd still love you."

"Thank you, Mom."

They hugged with all the unconditional love they felt for one another. Dillan already felt better.

Nick and Ben Coggwell walked in from the grocery store seeing Linda and Dillan's embrace. They both looked a little taken aback at the sight of the two hugging in the middle of the living room couch.

"Is everything okay?" Ben asked, setting down a mountain of groceries on the kitchen island.

"Everything's great," Linda said, getting up to greet her husband as Nick plopped on the couch with Dillan. He removed his hat and ran a hand through his short blonde hair.

"What's going on, sis?"

"Shit sucks." Dillan had no idea how much Nick knew and wasn't about to spill her guts. She sighed and rested her head on the arm of the couch, still sniffling.

"Yeah, Erika told me about it," he said.

"About what?"

"That Landi broke whatever you guys had off and chose Beth."

Dillan frowned, a bit confused. Landi had only "broken up" with her less than an hour ago.

"Yeah, when did you find out?" she asked, as nonchalantly as possible.

"The other day."

Dillan's mind spun. Nothing made sense anymore. Had Landi made the decision and blabbed to everyone but her about it? That sounded completely uncharacteristic of him. He would never do that. Not her Landi.

"Which totally blows. You guys are so cute together. You seemed really happy."

Dillan was still distracted, trying to understand the ridiculousness of everything.

"I've got a shitload of single friends who'd love to date you, so...just let me know."

"Okay, little brother," she said, playfully kicking him. "Thanks for the info."

All Dillan wanted to do was lay around and feel sorry for herself but Linda insisted that they have a mother daughter cooking extravaganza. She forced Dillan to get up and cook dinner with her, which turned out to be funner than Dillan had anticipated. They bounced around to tunes being silly in the Coggwell kitchen. By the time they all sat down for a big traditional family dinner, Dillan was feeling a hundred times better.

After dessert, Nick went off to Erika's while Dillan and her parents sat in the living room to flip through the five hundred plus cable channels.

She did her best to pay attention to the television and how great the evening had gone but annoyingly Dillan's mind kept going back to worry, guilt...and Landi. Her mother picked up on her discomfort, grabbing Dillan, a bottle of wine and some blankets for the back porch. They sat in the middle of the lawn and stared up at the stars, passing Merlot back and forth as crickets sang their summer songs.

Dillan took a sip of wine and looked up into the

night sky, her stomach uneasy.

"I think I'm going to tell him…everything," she said.

"That's a good idea."

"I don't think we can stay apart. It's just so unnatural. Even if I have to be his mistress, I will."

Her mother took a swig from the bottle then handed it to Dillan.

"This is probably going to embarrass the shit out of you but I'm just so relieved that you had sex. I was so afraid that you'd never be able to enjoy it again."

Dillan chuckled. "You're telling me."

"Was it amazing?"

"I'm not going to have this conversation with you, Mom."

"Oh, come on," she patted Dillan's leg as if that would help coax it out of her.

"Yes, it was fantastic, mind blowing, knock your f'n socks off incredible, okay?"

Linda laughed with a mischievous twinkle in her eye. "Now I get to tell you about *my* sex life."

"Um, I have to go…" Dillan began to get up. "I've got a meeting…"

Linda pulled her back into her chair as the two laughed, continuing their evening bond in the dark.

After a half bottle of wine at midnight, Dillan decided to crash in her old bed for the night. As soon as her head hit the fresh, linen-scented pillow she was out like a pile of bricks – until her bladder woke her up. She cursed herself for drinking too much, went to the bathroom and was about to creep back to her room when shuffling downstairs raised her curiosity. She didn't think too much of it until the phone rang throughout the house, startling her. Her mother's voice ended the phone's ringing but she couldn't hear a thing, so she made her way downstairs in the dark to see what was up. The kitchen sink light was on along with the entryway lights temporarily blinding her. To her surprise, her mother was wearing a light jacket with purse in hand ready to leave.

"Mom? Where are you going?"

"Go back to sleep honey, everything's fine." She looked frantic… and was lying.

"What's going on?"

"Jan's on her way to the hospital. I'm going to meet her and Landi there."

Dillan's stomach wrenched. "Is Jan okay?"

"She's in unbearable pain."

"Do you need my help?"

"I don't think so, sweetie."

Dillan sighed, trying to think through her sleepiness.

"Go get some rest and I'll update you in the morning. Everything's going to be fine. They'll probably just get her on some stronger pain meds and watch her for a little while."

Dillan nodded, not really sure if she agreed or not, then watched her mother open the door.

"Wait! I'm coming with you." She grabbed a hooded sweatshirt from the hall closet and found an old pair of flip-flops.

There was no way she was going to let Landi watch his mom suffer alone – not this time.

Walking through the hospital at three in the morning wearing a hoodie, her dad's t-shirt and a pair of Nick's boxers, Dillan felt like a combination of a zombie and a hobo. The bright lights made her feel even wackier

200

than she already did. Her head was hazy and she was a little dizzy, but somehow adrenaline kept her awake. She walked through the craziness of the emergency room, her mom at her side, looking around for Landi or Jan.

"I'm going to ask a nurse where she is," Linda said.

Dillan watched her mom walk to the nurse's station. Nothing much was going on there so she took a few steps and nosily looked around. She glanced down a hallway of glass-curtained rooms. Her heart skipped a beat, then sunk.

Landi sat just outside a room in the hallway, his head in his hands looking down at the floor. He looked up, directly in front of him, and then down again, his leg twitching nervously.

Even though he seemed completely exhausted and stressed out, Dillan found him adorably attractive. His disheveled hair, old t-shirt and beat up jeans only intensified the feeling.

She watched him for a couple of seconds, and then let her legs carry her his way. It wasn't until she sat down in the chair right beside him that he looked up at her, stunned.

"Dillan?"

She smiled at him, trying to convey her affection, adoration and sympathy. He seemed to get the message but it only made him appear sadder. Tears trickled down his face. Dillan wanted to make him feel better so she placed her hand on his.

"Landi."

"What are you doing here?" He wiped away any trace of tears from his face, breaking their physical connection.

"I stayed at my mom's..."

"There you are, what's going on?" Linda's face and tone oozed concern.

"She's having some tests done right now," Landi said. "I've been waiting for a while."

"Are you okay?"

"No."

Linda shifted from concerned to uncomfortable. "I'm going to go see if I can find some coffee. You guys want anything?"

Dillan shook her head, realizing Landi was too.

Linda disappeared and silence took over.

Dillan was unsure of what to say so she sat quietly, trying to think of the next best thing to talk about.

"I really thought she would be with me forever," Landi admitted.

Dillan took in a breath, then looked into his eyes, wanting to say something wise and comforting but nothing came out.

"It's eating her alive, from the inside out," his voice cracked. "I don't know what to do. I feel so God damned helpless." He stood and took a couple steps, then paced back.

Dillan stood up and caught him in a hug.

"I'm sorry," she whispered, holding on tightly as he reciprocated, gently embracing her back. He held her head to his chest as the other hand rested on the small of her back. It was a simple loving hold Dillan hadn't experienced since the last time he'd held her that way. She melted into him, feeling their love grow. It seemed nothing could keep them apart no matter how painful or difficult.

The door to Jan's room opened, breaking their embrace. A couple of nurses along with a big rolling

202

machine came out. Landi looked hopeful.

"You can go on in, she's resting."

"What's going on?" Landi asked. "Is everything all right? When will we get results?" He bombarded the nurses with questions, intent on getting information, while Dillan wandered into Jan's room.

She looked peaceful with her eyes closed, snuggled beneath a blue hospital blanket. Her thin dirty blonde hair was pulled back in a ponytail accentuating her gaunt face. An IV was embedded in her wrist attached to a hanging bag of saline nearby. Dillan took a few cautious steps toward her when her eyes opened. A big, almost goofy smile spread across her face.

"Did I drag you out of bed, too?" she asked, reaching her hand out for Dillan.

"No, I just came along for the ride."

Jan grabbed her hand and gave it a surprisingly strong squeeze.

"Are you feeling better?"

"Oh yeah, morphine works wonders."

Dillan chuckled as Jan's eyes went to the door.

"What are you so sad about?" asked Jan.

Landi walked in looking like he'd been through hell and back.

"You've got this sweet, beautiful woman to look at and all you can do is mope around?"

"I see you're back to your old jolly self," he said, lightening a little.

"Who are you calling old?"

"I brought you coffee anyway," Linda said walking in with three styrofoam cups. She handed two off to Dillan and Landi then bent over Jan, placing a hand atop hers. The two talked amongst themselves like the old friends they were as Dillan looked at Landi. The things she had said to him earlier that day had been eating at her since the incident, but it was a million times worse with him standing before her. She hoped he understood that when she said she was sorry, it was meant in a lot of ways.

His eyes wandered to hers as he took a sip of coffee. Her stomach fluttered.

"When are you two going to get over all the bullshit and just get together already?" Jan blurted.

"Mom..."

"It kills me to see you suffering, both of you."

There was an awkward silence.

"Why don't you run along and spend the rest of the night together. I'll be just fine."

"Mom, it's almost five in the morning."

"It is?" Jan looked puzzled, making them laugh. "You might have had something there with that old thing."

Even though Dillan was exhausted and not in her right mind she was enjoying being with three people she loved. She and Landi sat beside one another in standard hospital chairs sipping coffee. Jan had been entertaining them all with stories and rambling for almost two hours.

By sunrise, Dillan found herself wrapped in Landi's arms half asleep as if it were completely natural. Nothing in the world was more comforting. Linda had to drag Dillan from her Landi cloak after saying a long goodbye to Jan who seemed as wide-awake as a lucid person on drugs could get. Just before leaving, Dillan planted a soft kiss on Landi's cheek. He was completely unaware of the kiss or her departure.

Clarity ♡

*W*here are you? Is your mom home yet? I'm going to Erika's.

Landi wanted to throw his phone after reading Beth's stupid text. Like she gave a shit about anyone or anything but herself.

"Beth, huh?" Jan asked from her spot in her oversized reclining chair near the front window. Daylight lit up the room including Jan's face, which was much more relaxed. Landi smiled at his mom, glad to see her in her home setting versus the hospital. She'd been released that morning but he'd stayed with her all day as they rested and kept each other company.

"How'd you guess?"

"By the infuriated expression on your face."

Landi grinned.

"You deserve better."

"I know."

"I can't stand the thought of you having a child with that wretched woman." Jan shook her head. "And you know how bad I want grandbabies."

"What do you want for dinner?" Landi asked, shoving his phone between the couch cushions as if it would wipe the whole situation away. "Should we order something?"

"*I'm* sure as heck not cooking," she said with a smirk.

He watched his mom thumb through her gardening magazine. He saw the wise, strong beauty that radiated from her being. It reminded him of Dillan and how stubborn they both could be. He still couldn't believe she'd actually shown up at the hospital to support him and his mother, especially after he'd ripped her heart out. The gesture spoke volumes about just how much she truly cared for him. Unconditionally.

Then he remembered words that had been gnawing at him, *"...that's the reason I broke up with you all those years ago."*

He still didn't understand. Why would she not tell him about a pregnancy? What did that have to do with her scars? His obsessing only made him feel worse.

"Mom? Do you know what happened to Dillan?" he blurted.

His mother looked up from her magazine, stared at him for a moment and then set it aside. "I'm assuming you're talking about the reason she left you?"

Landi nodded. "Yes. I know about her scars and a pregnancy but nothing else. It's killing me. I've tried so hard to be respectful but the more details I get the more confused I am."

Jan sighed and removed her reading glasses.

"Have you asked Dillan?"

"Yes, several times. She gets defensive and shuts down."

Silence filled the room.

"Are you sure you want to know?" Jan asked.

He nodded.

Jan appeared apprehensive. She took a drink of iced tea then looked at her son.

"I only know because Linda told me – she needed to talk to someone about it. But as she did with me, I tell you this in confidence. What you do with it is your choice."

A knot formed in Landi's stomach. "I understand."

Jan took a moment before beginning.

"When Dillan was in college she went to a party with some girl friends in a remote part of town. I guess there were older men there. It wasn't a typical college gathering." Jan paused briefly as Landi's insides wrenched. "Dillan was drugged and led into the woods where she was brutally beaten and raped. She was abandoned and left for dead but a Good Samaritan found her. They took her to the hospital…"

Landi couldn't catch his breath. His entire body shook. Images of Dillan being tortured consumed him, causing waves of sickness he couldn't fight. He wiped cold sweat from his brow struggling to breathe.

"Are you okay?" Jan asked.

"Go on."

"She was in such bad shape that she went into surgery and was hospitalized for a week."

Landi was ready to kill the son of a bitch that tortured his girl.

"As if that wasn't bad enough, she became pregnant from the rape…which is why she broke up with you."

Landi's mind went back to that phone call – the one that changed it all.

"…I don't love you anymore, I'm in love with someone else! Don't you get it? I'm sick of you. I want to be with

207

someone different! Don't ever call me again!"

"But she miscarried..."

She had broken his heart to protect him. The realization was unbelievable. She hadn't found anyone at all. She did it because she loved him. *Loved* him...

Landi stood up.

"Where are you going?" Jan asked, suddenly alarmed.

"I have to see her."

With fists clenched, Landi got into his truck and tore off of Collister Drive toward Dillan's townhome. He couldn't believe what an idiot he'd been – how terribly he'd treated her. If only he'd known. Everything would have been different. But he knew now and he'd never doubt her again.

By the time he reached her door, he was on the verge of tears – angry, relieved and overwhelmed. He wasn't sure which emotion to grasp.

Dillan appeared in her comfy shorts and a tank top with her hair in a knot atop her head. Adorable.

"Hey..." Was all that escaped her mouth before he kissed it with all the love and passion he felt. A force field of intensity surrounded them.

"Wha?"

"I love you," he said, still nibbling on her lips.

"I love you, too."

They made eye contact for a split second before falling into another kissing spell. Landi kicked the door shut as they ravaged each other with lips locked. Dillan unbuckled his pants and quickly removed his t-shirt as he ran his hands all over her body. He was aroused the moment he saw her. He lifted her tank top off and kissed her neck as clothes fell to the floor leaving a trail in the hallway. By the time they reached the bed they were naked and winded, all consumed in each other. Nothing else mattered. They teased, nipped and nibbled in mounds of soft blankets until their bodies became one, dancing in a rhythm of pleasure that was sacredly theirs.

When they were breathless, sweaty and spent, Dillan laid her head on Landi's chest and ran a hand through his hair. His heart fluttered. Everything about her was magical.

"What was that for?" she asked, lightly kissing his damp skin.

"I couldn't resist how fucking cute you are."

"Oh, yeah?" she said, giving him a big smile.

He stared back, getting lost in her soul. "I'll never leave you again – ever. You've always been the one and I'm not going to let anyone or anything get in the way of that. I don't care what it takes."

Tears welled in her happy eyes. "Really?"

"Really."

"Okay, but I need to tell you…"

"I already know."

She tilted her head, causing blonde waves to tickle his chest. "You do?"

He nodded.

"Everything?"

"Unfortunately, yes."

"Oh." Her brows wrinkled. She was worried.

"But it only makes me love you more."

She lightened for a minute, then grew serious. "Do you understand why I felt I had no choice? I had to hurt you to protect you. I knew that if you found out what happened to me you'd try to kill my attacker. And I didn't want you to see me like that – I was such a mess, Landi. Then when I found out I was pregnant I knew I had to lie to

209

you. There was no way I was going to drag you through that mess. I wanted you to live a happy, normal life…"

"Di, none of that would have mattered. I understand why you did it but you didn't have to."

"Yes, I did," she looked into his eyes. "You promise you don't hate me?"

He rolled her over and kissed her pouty mouth. "God, I hate you so much I just want to kiss you," he teased, kissing her face and chest. Dillan laughed and begged him to stop, which only made him want to do it more.

Punchline ♡

"**A**www."

Dillan had her two best friends swooning like teenagers after explaining the latest development in the Landi and Dillan drama.

"So, what exactly are you guys going to do about Beth and that whole situation?" Tyann asked. "Have you talked about it?"

"Yeah, she's supposed to be going to the doctor next week. Landi's going to live with me and let her stay in the house until…well, you know." Dillan felt weird just talking about it. Their dilemma wasn't the ideal situation but Dillan didn't care – as long as she and Landi had each other they would be okay.

The women finally made it to the front of the fu-fu coffee joint line where Dillan watched Tyann order a large dulce de leche frozen coffee. Dillan made a smart-ass comment about her not being the only one that could be pregnant then ordered herself a fruity tropical smoothie for a change. Terry skipped her usual and got a small tin of peppermints.

"Terr, you're not going to get anything?" Tyann asked, almost offended.

She shrugged. "I don't feel like it right now."

Dillan and Tyann got their drinks and then the three found a table near the corner window where they could gossip and watch the puffy white clouds go by. Terry popped a mint in her mouth as Dillan and Tyann leisurely sipped their drinks.

"So, what's new with you two?" Dillan asked Tyann, glad to get off the subject of herself.

"Jason's been working longer hours so I picked up a couple more classes at the studio."

"More classes?"

"I don't want to be sitting at home waiting around. And it's not like I can't just leave when I need to. I've got plenty of staff."

Dillan raised an eyebrow. "How does Jason feel about that?"

"Good, other than being a little worried that when I come home I'll be too tired to have sex."

Dillan chuckled. Terry smiled.

"We're going to spend the weekend together so we'll have plenty of time to catch up." Tyann grinned, satisfied with her bragging.

"Thanks for the visual," Dillan remarked. "How are you, Terr?"

"Tired." That was obvious. Despite her beautiful natural features and half styled auburn hair she looked terrible. Her eyes were red with slightly purple half moons. Her cheeks were flushed and her skin was a bit clammy. She even looked a couple pounds lighter, which wasn't good for Terry since she was already on the thin side.

"Are you okay?" Dillan asked, realizing just how sick her friend appeared.

Terry shook her head as tears welled up in her weary eyes.

"Terr?"

"I broke it off with Charlie," she admitted.

Dillan and Tyann exchanged a stunned expression.

"Why? I thought things were going really good with you guys."

"It was…" Her gaze was distant. "I just can't put him through all of this anymore. It's not fair."

"But I thought you had an understanding?" Dillan asked, wondering how Charlie was handling it. "He knew it wasn't going to be anything more than physical, right?"

"Right."

"Well, what's the problem?"

She looked down at the table, then back up. Melancholy was written all over her. "I'm getting too attached."

Dillan had to keep from smiling. "Which isn't good because...?"

"I'm still married and tangled up in this mess with Jesse. The last thing I need right now is to get caught up with another player."

Tyann nodded. "I agree that you don't need to be starting another serious relationship right now but Charlie makes you happy, doesn't he? I don't see anything wrong with having a little distraction, especially if it's only temporary."

"I don't need any men in my life right now." Terry insisted. "I just want to be alone."

There was an abrupt pause as Dillan and Tyann

sipped on their drinks.

"You're still not speaking to Jesse?" Dillan asked.

"Nope, other than making arrangements where Tibby is concerned."

"How did Charlie take the news?"

"He seems a little bummed but understands."

Dillan wondered if Charlie's feelings for Terry had grown since the last time she talked to him about it. If so, he had to be heartbroken. She was wondering why he hadn't told her about it when Terry started crying.

"I'm sorry," she said, wiping tears from her cheeks.

Dillan gave her a big hug then placed a supportive hand on her back, patiently waiting for her to go on.

"I hate Jesse," she blurted. "I HATE him. Why did I choose the biggest dickhead in Boise to marry and have a child with? WHY?" She sobbed. "I don't know what to do. It's driving me CRAZY!" She stood and disappeared into the coffeehouse bathroom while Dillan and Tyann stared at each other in shock.

"Oh my goodness." Dillan's stomach sank. She wanted to help Terry but had no idea how.

"That poor thing, she's been through a lot."

"What do we do?"

Tyann looked as if she were scheming. "Talk to Charlie."

Exactly what Dillan had in mind.

After an extravagant weekend shopping spree at the mall, primarily focused on Terry and the chickiest chick flick they could find, Dillan and Tyann had succeeded in lifting Terry's spirits. They went back to Tyann's, put on their sexy new swimsuits, then lounged around the pool drinking wine while listening to loud music in the hot afternoon sunshine.

Dillan call me – we need to talk.
Now! Charlie's text was not unexpected.

Dillan: Simmer down lover boy. I'll call
you later. I'm with Terry.

Charlie: Where are you? I'm coming
over.

As promised Charlie arrived not fifteen minutes
later. He walked through the back fence in surf shorts, a
tank top and flip flops looking much more serious than his
usual self.

"Wuz up?" he asked, plopping right beside Terry
who smiled into his eyes. Tyann and Dillan exchanged a
grin, already knowing the answer to the question: They
were madly in love with one another.

"So, what the hell *is* up?" Dillan asked, raising her
sunglasses to look at him from her lounge chair.

"Di, you're not going to believe this."

Charlie had them all leaning in with curiosity.

"So I went to a restaurant last night. It was kinda
late but I just needed a few beers to chill, right?"

Dillan nodded, un-amused.

"This chick comes up and starts talking to me…"

Terry stiffened.

"…she proceeds to tell me that her boyfriend just
broke up with her but she has this grand plan to get him
back by taking his house and all of his money… and how
she's already making his life hell because he thinks he's
going to have to take care of her."

Dillan was locked in, not quite getting the
punchline.

"So I play along and I ask her, what's your name?
She says, Beth. Then I ask, what's your ex's name?"

This time Charlie widened his eyes at her.

"Landi."

Tyann gasped so loud it nearly echoed. Dillan began to shake as the realization soaked in. Charlie took out his phone and flashed his contacts in her face.

"*Beth* gave me her number."

"Oh my God," Terry's words were muffled by the hand over her mouth.

"Yeah." Charlie sat back in his chair for the first time eyeing Terry's bikini clad body.

"That bitch!" Dillan yelled, bubbling with anger. If Beth had been in front of her she'd have punched her square in the face. Dillan was blind with fury, unable to fathom the fact that Beth had been lying and screwing with her and Landi the entire time. How dare she! How could anyone do something so selfish and conniving? Dillan had never been so pissed in her entire life. She was ready to destroy.

"Wait, so she's not pregnant?" Terry asked. "What about the test? Someone is."

"Who gives a shit? I'm going to kill her!" Dillan stood from her chair and began frantically hunting for her shorts and tank top. She'd track Beth down and give her a piece of reality.

"Whoa, slow down, Killer." Charlie stood before her and placed his hands over her shoulders. "I know you're pissed but we've got to do this the right way."

"You better have a good plan."

He smirked. "Have I ever let you down?"

Corner Booth ♡

It was just like a scene from a movie. His heart pounded, adrenaline pumped. This man was on a mission. He walked through the doors of Sal's Steakhouse with a bag in one hand and manila folder in the other. Landi couldn't remember the last time he felt so exhilarated. He was about to take back his life and sanity.

Sal's was buzzing for a Sunday evening. Every seat at the bar was taken along with most of the restaurant tables. The fireplaces were blazing, music was wafting and mouth-watering smells pumped into the dining area from the kitchen. If he were there for any other reason he'd be tempted to grab a bite but not tonight.

Landi shot a cute smile at the hostesses hovering over the front desk. They giggled and smiled, thinking nothing of him walking past them without a peep. They knew him all too well – a good thing. He walked through the tables toward the corner booth near the window facing the hills.

There she was.

Charlie had ditched his hat for the occasion. He wore a t-shirt and jeans for the "date". That charming Charlie. Beth sat beside him beaming in all of her evil glory – hair down, a full on mask of makeup, revealing top. His stomach churned at the sight. The fact that he was ever with the girl made him sick.

The moment Beth caught his eyes color drained from her face. She looked ready to vomit at any moment. Good.

"Hey guys," Landi sat on the edge of the booth across from them cool and calm as if he were meant to be there. He was more than ready for this.

"Uh...I...was..." Beth stuttered, still reeling. She looked at Charlie whose face was blank, then back at Landi.

"Hi, Beth. How are you feeling?" Landi asked, boring his eyes into hers. "Oh, wait. You're not pregnant. How could I forget?"

She swallowed.

"So a couple of things," he opened the manila folder and shoved a document in front of her face. "This piece of paper is a restraining order telling you to stay away from me, my property and Dillan. Unless you want to go to jail I suggest you don't come near us."

Her jaw opened but nothing came out.

Landi pulled the paper away and set it back in its folder then grabbed the bag he'd set on the floor and held it up.

"This is the rest of your shit. Some of it accidentally got damaged. Sorry." He threw it on the table in front of her.

"And you might want to call your parents. Someone pretty convincing filled them in on your alcohol abuse and reckless behavior. You probably need some professional help."

Beth's face began to fill in with color – and rage. He had finally gotten to her.

"I think that's about it. Have a nice life."

Landi and Charlie stood leaving Beth writhing. She was about to blow.

Just before walking away Landi couldn't resist.

"Oh, and one more thing... don't hit on my friends."

As he and Charlie walked away Landi swore he heard a loud squeal of frustration coming from the corner booth near the window facing the hills.

♡

"Are you okay?" Dillan's caring words, loving hug and soft lips caused Landi to momentarily forget about his courageous act. He'd barely taken a step into her townhome before getting all consumed by his woman. He breathed his sweet Dillan in, holding her close.

"Get those two away from each other!" Jason yelled from the couch. He, Dillan, Tyann and Terry had been lounging in Dillan's townhome patiently waiting for them to return. A big bowl of popcorn and snacks sat on the coffee table along with glasses of wine, soda and beer.

"What happened?" Tyann asked, nestled up to her husband.

Dillan and Landi joined Tyann and Jason on the couch as Terry and Charlie shared a kiss and blanket on the floor.

"It was awesome!" Charlie exclaimed. "Everything went perfectly. You should have seen the look on her face."

219

"Really?" Jason asked, wide-eyed and curious. "She bought the restraining order bit?"

"Yep." He and Charlie told their friends exactly what had happened down to the smallest details. It seemed they were all relieved when a peaceful silence filled the room.

"She got what she deserved," Tyann remarked, throwing a handful of popcorn into her mouth. "Do you think Nick has figured out that Erika's the one who's really pregnant?"

"I think he's in denial," Dillan said. "I might have to have a little birds, bees and babies talk with him."

Charlie burst into laughter. "Good luck with that."

Landi admired Dillan as warmth filled his chest. He was overwhelmingly happy... finally free to love the woman who'd stolen his heart ten long years ago when he was just a naïve thirteen-year-old boy.

"Let's crack open those marshmallows and fire up the pit." Charlie said, helping Terry up. "We can celebrate with s'mores!"

Landi, Jason and Charlie went to the patio to fire up the pit while the women collected blankets, snacks and beverages. It was a beautiful summer night. A bright full moon illuminated lush grass and trees while crickets chirped in the distance. Smells of dewy shrubbery wafted throughout the air, mixing with campfire smoke. They broke out the blankets and chairs and stared into the fire, mesmerized by its flames. Landi held Dillan close as she nestled up to him in their blanket bundle.

The friends laughed and teased, getting drowsy from the warmth of the fire and one another.

Landi had just swallowed another gooey marshmallow when Dillan turned and smiled at him with a sparkle in her eye.

"Is it true?" she asked. "That I have you all to myself? Could it be?"

"You always had me, Di."

"I know," she grinned. "Because you always had me."

Babies n' Such ♥

"**H**oly shit! Look at that rock!" Terry grabbed Dillan's hand to gawk at the ring adorning her finger. Diamonds glittered in the spring sunshine.

"Isn't it beautiful?" Tyann asked, rubbing her big round belly.

"It's perfect," Dillan said. "For us."

She glanced at her fiancé who smiled at her from his seat on their brand new patio.

"I'm jealous," Terry said. "New home, new ring…you probably have a set of twins on the way, too."

"Not yet, but we're working on it," Dillan grinned at Landi getting a raised eyebrow. "And don't act like you're unhappy, Miss Smitten With Charlie. Before long you guys will be married and popping them out."

"Actually…" Terry's pink cheeks flamed red.

"No?!?!" Tyann barked.

"I've been meaning to tell you…I'm having a kid – with Charlie."

Dillan and Tyann gasped in unison.

"Does Jesse know?"

"Yeah, but it's okay. I think he's genuinely happy for me...*finally.*"

"Wow."

"It's all on you now, Di."

As if she and Landi weren't already feeling the pressure. Jan and Linda were dying for grandchildren and reminded them constantly. Dillan was content with everything exactly as it was. She and Landi were soaking in every second with each other even after eight months. She still couldn't get enough of him. A baby would only add to their love – but she wasn't in a hurry.

"What are you three gossiping about over here?"

Linda and Jan approached them - all grins and smiles.

"Babies and such."

"Oh God, don't get them started." Dillan said, thinking of her brother and his newborn. "Have you heard from Nick today, mom?"

"Yes, they're doing fine. We're going to go visit him later and see little Flower."

"Only your brother would name a baby Flower," Tyann remarked, rolling her eyes.

"I think it's pretty," said Terry, off somewhere in the clouds.

Charlie, Jason and Landi emerged from their shade on the patio to the grassy lawn where the women stood. The looks Tyann and Dillan gave Charlie were far from obscure.

"What's the deal?" he laughed. "Why am I getting the evil eye?"

"Don't act like you don't know," Tyann teased.

He shrugged.

"Love the new home, guys," Jason said, still carefully eyeing details. "But I do have a few remodel ideas."

"I'm sure you do." Dillan smirked. "So do I. Let's get together and chat."

"Dinner?"

"Deal."

This time Landi and Tyann exchanged looks.

"What's that noise?"

A piercing sound came from the house, along with a faint smell.

"Didn't you have cookies in the oven?" Landi asked.

"Oh, no!" Dillan ran through the sliding glass door to the kitchen and opened up the oven.

A billow of smoke came tumbling out.

Landi turned the oven off then grabbed a towel and began waving it at the fire alarm. The beeping stopped as Dillan removed the charcoal mounds with her red paisley oven mitt – coordinating, of course.

When the urgency of the moment subsided, they stood staring at each other – slightly frazzled.

"Yum, those look amazing," Landi said, trying to keep a straight face.

"Yeah? Why don't you eat one?"

"Um, you first."

They burst out laughing, smudging burnt cookie lines all over one another.

"At least I didn't paint the living room baby poop brown." Dillan teased.

Landi attacked her with tickles and pokes. "You said you liked it."

"I do. I love it because you did it."

Dillan nuzzled Landi's nose and gave him a sweet kiss.

"I love you, Goof."

"Ditto, Dill."

♡

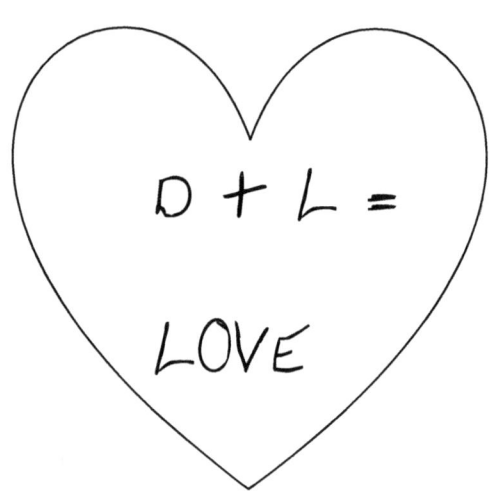

Meet Melissa ♡

Melissa Kline is a hopeless romantic and tends to see life through rose-colored glasses. She has an uncanny ability to find romance in any situation. Melissa loves to write quirky romance and chick-lit for women of all ages. She enjoys reading romance almost as much as she loves writing about it. "Life is lighter when you add a pinch of love!" says Melissa. Find out more about Melissa's continuing journey at **MelissaKlineAuthor.com**

Acknowledgments ♡

Many thanks to my beautiful writing family, the Rocky Mountain Women Writers, for encouraging, supporting and believing in me through every step of the writing process.

Thank you Francelia Belton-Briscoe, a.k.a Mama Bear for keeping me on track!

Thanks to my talented soul sister Mishelle Crutchfield for always being my rock and sounding board. Your strength and courage is inspiring!

Thanks to my partner-in-crime Melissa Ingram for the laughs, hugs and positive encouragement.

To sweet Marlaina Kline for always believing in me through life's ups and downs. Thank you for supporting me from the very beginning!

Thank you Kris Jordan for your honesty, enthusiasm and encouragement...even though romance isn't your thing. ;)

Thanks to Carmen Swick for always being so uplifting and positive.

Thanks to E. Jeanie Barr for your die-hard dedication to romance and love. You're so very special!

Thank you Sherri Jennings for your time and willingness to help with this project. You helped me grow as a writer!

Thanks to my mother, Sue Foster, for your love, faith and understanding. I love you!

To my boys, CK2, CK3 and Liam for being patient while I write – I love you! And thanks to my beloved Pops for always being my biggest fan. Your love, support and encouragement means so much. The convertible is on its way.

More Books by Melissa Kline

My Beginning – Dystopian Young Adult Fiction

After a devastating plague, children are sealed in institutions. Ivory dreams of the outside world and risks everything to escape with her forbidden love. They explore a new world, and find life unexpectedly thriving – but also a war raging. Will they survive?

Storm – Contemporary Young Adult Fiction

Storm enjoys skateboarding, fixing broken electronics and building things with his hands. They distract him from the tormented thoughts surrounding the circumstances of his mother's death. But his problems can't be avoided forever...will Storm overcome his fears and reveal his long-held secrets?

Coming soon!

Arcane – Dystopian New Adult Fiction

Jett is surviving in a world where weather is violent and deadly. He's torn between love, family and life during his travels to rediscover the devastated land. What will he find?

For sneak peeks, book trailers and more go to MelissaKlineAuthor.com